TRAPPING, TURK

A Camper And Criminals Cozy Mystery

Book Twenty Eight

BY
TONYA KAPPES

TONYA KAPPES
WEEKLY NEWSLETTER

Want a behind-the-scenes journey of me as a writer?
The ups and downs, new deals, book sales, giveaways and more? I share it all! Join the exclusive Southern Sleuths private group today! Go to www.patreon.com/Tonyakappesbooks

As a special thank you for joining, you'll get an exclusive copy of my cross-over short story, *A CHARMING BLEND.* Go to Tonyakappes.com and click on subscribe at the top of the home page.

"Your friend Jerry Truman didn't help at all. He put my family in the poorhouse. He shut my dad's business down without even trying to let my dad recover." He spit out the words over his shoulder at me but kept walking.

"Your dad was selling liquor to minors." Abruptly, I stopped when he did so I didn't smack into him.

Slowly, he turned around and gave me the most evil look.

"Listen, I don't think you should be here any longer." He fisted his hands and turned back around to keep going toward the greenhouse. "I'll tell Garrett to call you when I find him."

"You'll what?" I asked just as a dark cloud came over us and sprinkles of snow started to fall from the sky.

"This is why I left here." He stopped, threw his hands in the air, and looked up at the snow.

"What did you say about Garrett?" I asked.

"I told you to go," he said through gritted teeth and started to walk again. "I said"—his voice was a little louder—"I'll tell Garrett to call…"

There was a hesitation in his steps, and his eyes were forward.

I looked past him to see what had caught his attention and stopped him from finishing his sentence.

"Garrett!" He darted off in a sprint with his eyes on the greenhouse door that was propped open by Garrett Callis's body.

Lifeless body.

Garrett wasn't going to call anyone.

Anymore.

CHAPTER ONE

It was a whiff. A brief moment really. Enough of a moment that it got my attention and took me right back to the small kitchen of my childhood home in Perrysburg, Kentucky.

A far cry from where I stood at the kitchen sink at the Milkery, where my hands were busy peeling the shells off hard-boiled eggs.

"Be sure you knock it against the sink all the way around the outside before you start to peel." Mary Elizabeth gave me the side-eye when she must've seen me staring out the window. "I know my hard-boiled eggs are delicious, but they look good when you have the nice and shiny smooth outside. Especially when they are sitting in the little egg holder of the antique china of my mama's. Which one day soon will be yours." Her voice trilled with excitement.

"Hank and I have no place to put any extra dishes," I told her, knowing she was going to try to pass off all her china, vases, family cloth napkins, and things I'd need to host a southern dinner party, which was not on my radar even if I didn't live in a campervan.

I picked up another hard-boiled egg from the pan of cold water. As I knocked it along the ceramic sink, I carefully rotated it to make sure it was cracking all the outside of the shell.

"You'll have to find a place. You are also going to have to get a bigger refrigerator to keep a frozen coffee cake, so when you do have company drop by, you will have something good for them to eat on a beautiful serving plate." She sighed happily at the thought of my impending nuptials to Hank Sharp even though the wedding wouldn't be until the next year. "Which does make me wonder if you two have talked about a real house."

"Nope. We've not discussed anything about the wedding, though I do think I've narrowed down my bridesmaids." I knew I had to give Mary Elizabeth something to chew on to get her through the holidays.

The bell over the front door of the Milkery sounded, signaling a new bed-and-breakfast guest for her.

"Hold that thought." She picked up the edges of her apron and wiped her hands clean before she reached around to untie it, threw it on the kitchen table, looked into the microwave as a mirror to make sure she was presentable, and darted out of the kitchen to meet her new guests.

The back door swung open. Abby Fawn Bonds, my sister-in-law, peeked inside.

"Knock, knock. Anyone home?" Abby's eyes darted around.

"Thank goodness you are here." I tossed the broken eggshells in the empty coffee tin Mary Elizabeth had given me so she could use the shells to compost and put in the Milkery garden to help fertilize the soil. "Mary Elizabeth has some dishes for you and Bobby Ray."

"Oh no, you don't. We've already turned them down. We told her it was only right for the daughter to get them." She snickered and pulled off her coat. "It's turned downright cold. I think we skipped right over fall and went straight to winter."

"Fine by me." I gave her a hug after she'd hung her coat up on the hook next to the door. "I'm so ready for the season to slow down." I laughed. "I never thought I'd say it, but I need a break."

After I got Happy Trails Campground, the campground I owned and lived in, up and running as one of the best campgrounds in the state, we were always packed. Even during the winter months, but it was those few months where the more experienced campers came because it wasn't as packed as the seasonal months. They didn't require all my attention, and over the last couple of camping seasons, we'd been swamped, leaving me little time to think about, much less plan, a wedding.

"If the weather is going to be anything like the almanac says, we are in for big winter storms, starting on Thanksgiving." She sighed and walked over to wash her hands before picking up an egg to help me.

"That's just a few days away." I glanced back out the window and looked up at the skyline on top of the mountains of the Daniel Boone National Forest. "How many more do you think we need?"

"She told me there's about fifteen guests." She looked down at the bowl of unshelled eggs. "This is a lot more than fifteen guests."

"Keep shelling." I giggled and picked one up. I was able to peel them while looking out at the orange, red, gold, and green colors dotting the mountainside.

Fall in and around the park was a picture like nothing else I'd ever seen. I certainly didn't take it for granted. Autumn was my favorite season. Hank and I hadn't made a true wedding date, but as the fall season was quickly passing by with the first snowfall of the year, my heart was being tugged to plan a gorgeous fall wedding, which meant we'd have to wait almost an entire year.

It was fine. It wasn't like either of us was going anywhere. Hank and Jerry Truman had started their own private investigation service, keeping him busy. Happy Trails Campground was literally booked solid for the next two years, which had me tied up so the year would fly by. I wouldn't tell my thoughts to Mary Elizabeth or even Abby just yet. It was only fair of me to consider Hank and his thoughts. Discussing it with him first would be the best thing to do.

The faint whiff of paprika circled me again, taking me right back to my childhood, where I stood on a small stool next to my mama, not Mary Elizabeth but my birth mother, and helped her sprinkle the top of her hard-boiled eggs with the spice.

"There she goes again." I heard Mary Elizabeth's voice behind me. "She's been daydreaming all morning."

"You okay?" Abby leaned over the sink and looked at me. "You seem distracted."

"It's funny how you get one little smell of something and a whole host of feelings come sweeping in with a flood of memories." I put the egg down and picked up the paprika. "This reminds me of my mom when I was a little girl and doing this exact same thing."

"Then we won't use it." Abby plucked it from my hands and hurried off toward the butler's pantry. "Anything that will make you sad will not be used for this Thanksgiving."

"It's fine. It's fine." I shrugged. "I love my memories of my mom when I get them. They've started to fade."

This was something I knew would naturally occur as I got older. The memories of my parents and siblings along with the sound of their voices, something I'd tried so hard to keep, were starting to fade or take on a different image than what was true. The facts were the facts. They were deceased. I was adopted by Mary Elizabeth when I was a teenager, and now close to thirty, I'd been with Mary Elizabeth longer than my birth family.

"I too recently had some of those memories." Abby nibbled on her lip. Her brows furrowed. "You can't imagine my shock when Lester Hager walked into the library. Just seeing him again reminded me of all the work I'd done for the church at the library when he was the preacher."

"Are you talking about Lester, Betts's husband?" Dawn Gentry came into the kitchen.

"I know you've told this story a million times, but I've not heard it myself." Dawn indicated the gossip mill was running wild with the governor's recent pardon of two citizens of Normal, Kentucky.

"I'm not sure if you knew, but a few months ago, I'd gone to see Lester in the prison." I glanced at Abby and smiled.

We—Abby, Betts Hager, Dottie Swaggert, Queenie French, and I— were known as the Laundry Club Ladies. We were a group of best friends of different ages who loved to eat, read, and had a knack for sleuthing out criminals.

4

It was something we just so happened upon once during our book club, and now we were like those crime podcasts but real-life armchair detectives.

Unfortunately, Lester Hager was the Normal Baptist preacher who'd killed someone. It was for self-defense, but it was still a crime, and he was sent to life in prison until recently.

I continued, "I was snooping around and knew Lester might have some prison insider information." I grabbed the coffee carafe and headed over to the kitchen table to refill my mug from earlier.

Abby and Dawn gestured to me to fill their cups as we all took a seat at the table.

"Lester confided to me he'd been diagnosed with cancer and didn't have much longer to live." Though Lester did a horrific crime of taking someone's life, he was still a person, and I had felt awful for him. "He made me promise not to tell Betts, and for months, I would avoid her questioning me about seeing him, because he took her off his list of visitors."

It was one of the hardest things I'd ever had to do. Out of all the Laundry Club Ladies, Betts was probably the best friend and confidant of all of them. Just thinking about Lester's secret still made my heart hurt even though things had since changed.

"He thought if he took Betts off his list, she'd just forget about him, and then he'd die without her knowing what he'd passed from." The reasoning was ridiculous, but I only wanted what was best for my friend, so when Lester first presented this crazy notion, I kept it to myself.

Dawn held on to the mug with one hand while her other hand picked at the edges of her pixie cut. Her hair was coal black as were her clothes. She had on a pair of skinny black jeans, a black tank top, and a black leather jacket. She wore the jacket as more of a shirt than a jacket.

Dawn had stayed in Happy Trails Campground when one of her famous author clients was in town to write and escape the daily grind of fame. Dawn ended up forming an unlikely relationship with Mary Elizabeth. Neither of them lived here, but the Milkery, the local dairy farm, had become available to purchase. They went into business together and literally transformed the Milkery into an amazing working dairy farm with a bed-and-breakfast.

"One night, there was a knock at my campervan door." I laughed out loud, recalling the night. "Fifi and I thought it was Hank and Chester."

Fifi was my little poodle, and Chester was Hank's dog. Hank lived full-time in the campground, so it wasn't uncommon for them to venture over when they were out for a walk or couldn't sleep.

"I swung the door open, and there stood Lester and Grady Cox Jr." Without going into too much detail about Grady Cox Jr., I continued to tell her about Lester. "Lester told me the governor had pardoned both of them."

Grady Jr., who went by Junior, was a questionable pardon, but the governor didn't care. He was going out of office, and a lot of the pardons he'd made didn't make much sense, but I wasn't in politics nor did I want to be.

"Lester didn't have a place to go. Junior had me call Ava." I was talking about his mama, Ava Cox, a local attorney. "She rushed to the campground, and you know Dottie."

The three of us laughed.

"She had no idea who was driving so fast up the campground." I smiled. I couldn't get the images out of my head of Dottie running down the road of the campground toward my campervan with her red hair snugged up in those hot-pink curlers, cigarette smoke rolling out of her mouth, with her fuzzy housecoat and matching slippers on.

She looked like she was on fire.

"Ava took Junior home and left me there with Dottie, who was in major disbelief." I was shocked too. "Never in a million years did I ever think Lester or Grady Jr. would be pardoned."

"This is like one of those crime show stories that are so hard to believe." Dawn's brows lifted. She slowly shook her head and took a sip of the steaming hot coffee.

"It was crazy. Dottie had a million questions because she was hot on the cell phone, calling Al Hemmer." I groaned talking about Normal's sheriff. "Lester had all the paperwork, and he was in street clothes but super thin and just looked ill."

"I heard he has cancer." Abby pulled her foot onto the seat of the kitchen chair and hugged her bent leg. "Betts is taking care of him, and happily."

"She is. She's been taking him to treatment, though he'd resisted treatment at first." From what I understood, there wasn't a cure, but Lester and Betts were still God-fearing people who believed in miracles. "Betts keeps saying a mustard seed of hope."

"Still, it's crazy he showed up at your place." Dawn looked down the hall when she heard someone walking.

Mary Elizabeth stopped at the door and placed her hands on her hips.

"What do y'all think you're doing? Sittin' around like this when we have a Thanksgiving dinner to fix for the fifteen guests." She stuck her leg out wider. "Well? Get up."

"Was she like this when you were growing up?" Dawn teased.

"Worse." I stood up and wrapped my arms around Mary Elizabeth, giving her a nice hug before I went back to my egg-shelling job. "But I love her."

"If you love me so much, you will set a wedding date before I die," she muttered just loud enough for all of us to hear her.

"Before you die?" I rubbed my thighs. "Before I die. My legs are killing me."

"How is that going?" Abby asked and picked up her coffee to take a sip. She looked so cute in her long brown pigtails. Abby was the librarian at the Normal Public Library, and most days, she literally played the typical idea of how a librarian was portrayed with her hair pulled up in a tight bun or a swinging ponytail.

"I'm not sure, but I think Christine is very much enjoying the fact I am having a hard time keeping up." I was joking about Christine Watson.

She was the owner of the Cookie Crumble, and it was a well-known fact that I did enjoy her cookies very much. Too much.

When she dropped off the weekly cookies for the hospitality room at Happy Trails Campground, I did sneak a few of them to my camper so I could enjoy one daily with my own coffee. This time of the year especially. She made seasonal cookies, and hers were to die for.

They came at a cost. Calories and sugar. Not that I cared too much about gaining some weight. But I still had this image of me in a wedding dress since I was a teenager that didn't include me holding a cookie from the Cookie Crumble.

So to offset any unwanted health issues and have my cookie too, I'd taken Christine up on her offer to join her running group. Little did I know they were training for the upcoming Turkey Trot, a local 5k run where the proceeds went to local food banks, which was a much-needed charity around here.

"You've been running for a month or two now." Dawn leaned back with both hands around her mug.

"Each morning they make the run longer and longer. Don't get me started on the extra night runs." I sighed and looked at the clock. "Which I told Christine I'd meet her at the Cookie Crumble for an afternoon jog so we can all meet up at the Red Barn tonight."

"Yes. Bobby Ray is excited. He said he's met a lot of new guys that hung out with Joel." Abby was referring to Joel Grassel, the owner of Grassel's Garage, the local filling station and mechanic.

Bobby Ray worked for Grassel's Garage, and they'd become good friends.

"People around here are crazy about tonight's tradition." Mary Elizabeth could tell we were all about to leave, so she filled up our cups of coffee.

It was her way of nonchalantly keeping us there by telling us we had to finish our coffee. She didn't want us to leave even though she was busying herself by cleaning up the mess we'd made from all the pre-cooking we'd done.

"A few of my guests are in town just for tonight." She wiped down the kitchen counter and turned the water faucet on to clean out the dishrag before she wrung it out, laying it over the edge of the sink.

"Hank is too." I knew the annual reunion of locals coming in for the Thanksgiving holiday was a long-standing tradition held at the Red Barn Restaurant.

According to Hank, for years, everyone gathered there, talking about old times, good times, catching up, and it was something they all looked forward to. No matter what year they graduated from the local high school, they all gathered.

This was the first year I was able to go, and Hank was excited to introduce me to some of his friends who were coming into town that had long moved away, so getting in one of those extra runs with Christine made me feel like I could enjoy some of the great appetizers and a drink or two while Hank showed me off.

I snickered at the thought.

CHAPTER TWO

Thanksgiving was my favorite holiday. The day would be spent around people who had made my life amazing and full, the people I love and who love me. Most of them weren't family. They were friends.

Mary Elizabeth had already decided she would host a separate Thanksgiving for the guests a few days earlier so she could host a huge Thanksgiving for our friends and family on the grounds of the Milkery.

With the snow in the forecast, I wasn't sure what Mary Elizabeth had planned, and she didn't even acknowledge the possibility when I asked her. Instead of worrying about it, I was going to let myself go with the flow just as she appeared to be doing.

But the weather was far from rain.

"How was Mary Elizabeth?" Christine Watson asked. She stood at the glass display counter.

My eyes fixated on the rows of freshly baked cookies, muffins, and cakes, but my ears were open to listening to her.

"She was good. The Milkery bed-and-breakfast is fully booked, so that makes her happy. Not the income part but the feeling like she's got people to take care of." I looked up and watched Christine as she held a cookie sheet in one hand while using the spatula in the other hand to put the cookies on another baking tray resting on the cooling rack.

"You will have to try this one." The smile on her face made all the freckles across her nose expand. She put the tray down and tugged the hairnet off her head, letting her brown hair flow around her shoulders. "Dirty chai doughnuts!"

"Oh my goodness." I had to swallow all the saliva from just hearing the name. "What in earth is in them?"

The name sounded scary, but they looked amazing.

"Ginger, chai mix of course, cinnamon." She continued to rattle off all the ingredients just as though it were everyday language that I understood, but it amazed me how she could throw these spices together to make something that not only tasted so good but also looked pretty.

Her voice trailed off as she pushed through the swinging door from the shop into the kitchen.

"I'm grabbing my shoes," I heard her say as I paced back and forth, listening to the other customers order from one of Christine's employees.

Christine and her sister, Mallory, owned the Cookie Crumble. When they first opened the location here in Normal, Mallory was here a lot. Then they opened the one in Slade, Kentucky. It was going so well, Mallory worked there full-time, and now Christine was here full-time.

"Are you ready?" She came out totally transformed in her black running shorts, short-sleeved shirt, and bright-pink running shoes.

I got a glimpse of my reflection in the display case glass, making a note to stop by the Tough Nickel Thrift Shop to see what Buck might have in the way of running things.

"I am." I let go of a heavy sigh.

"That was a mighty big sigh." She nodded out the door where a few of the other runners from the group had stopped on their run to pick us up along the way. "You're doing great."

She pushed out the front door, and I followed her.

"Who's doing what?" Will Denning, Christine's longtime friend and the person in charge of the running group, stood there with his knee bent behind him. He had ahold of his shoe and stretched the front of his thigh.

"I was telling Mae that for a beginner, she's been doing great." Christine and a few of the others did their routine stretching to get them ready for the few-mile run ahead of us.

"Is something going on?" Will asked.

He was a physical trainer for the school sports and at a local nursing home, so he knew a few things about muscles and cramping.

"I thought after a few months of this, my thighs would stop hurting at some point." I bent over and rubbed them.

"Have you been doing the lunges like we talked about?" he asked and put his hands on his waist, gliding down into front lunges. "Come on. It'll help."

He gestured for me to mimic him. Instead of just me doing it, the entire group did it.

"See. We've got you." He smiled and led a few more leg stretches before he darted off like a jet. The rest took off after him, leaving me and Christine lagging behind.

"Really." I kept pace with her. "You go on and join them. I'll be fine."

"No way." The sound of her feet hit the pavement and married the sound of the crickets and the chirping birds along the curvy road of the Daniel Boone National Forest. "We are in this together. Tonight we can all talk about running and make people roll their eyes."

"Huh?" I got enough breath to question what she was talking about.

"The Red Barn reunion. You're going, right?" Christine was able to talk, ask questions, focus on a conversation, and not miss a beat or slow down. Her breath didn't even change.

I, on the other hand, had a hard time comprehending anything but sucking and gasping for air.

"Oh yeah." I had to mentally wrap my head around her question, focus on it while trying to keep my feet on the pavement, and not venture off the cliff on each side of the road. "Hank is pretty excited about seeing some old high school friends who are coming into town."

The sun was high in the sky, and my thoughts drifted to the campground, where I could see Dottie savoring that afternoon cup of coffee, snuggled up in one of the Adirondack chairs near the lake with a blanket over her legs to ward off the day's chill. She was talking to the guests who were just coming back from their afternoon hike on the trails surrounding Happy Trails.

"If only I didn't love your doughnuts so much," I grumbled.

"What?" Christine asked. She was a couple of steps ahead of me. "Did you say something about doughnuts?"

"I should be at the campground with a cup of coffee and a doughnut right now," I called and noticed the group ahead had veered off the blacktopped road and down into the woods.

"What are we doing?" I asked when I didn't know why we were going off the road. "I'm not built to do trail running."

Trail running and trail hiking were two very different things. My body was barely built for the hiking, and even then, I was liable to trip on the roots sticking up out of the ground. Could you imagine Mary Elizabeth's face if I fell and broke something? Possibly not healing for months.

She'd get put into a treatment facility for a nervous breakdown due to the fact I'd gone and hurt myself doing something I wasn't meant to do.

Trail run.

"It will help with endurance for the next couple of days leading up to the Turkey Trot." Was it bad that I found her being a little breathy made me the slightest bit happy?

Up ahead Will stood in the small space next to a tree and jogged in place, watching everyone run past.

"Are y'all okay back here?" He directed his question at me and Christine, but his eyes were focused solely on me.

"She's great," I got out before I sucked in another deep breath. "Me on the other hand is iffy," I teased, but it opened the door for him to continue to carry on the conversation while he jogged behind me.

"Running on the uneven trails is really good for glutes and quads." He was using his education as a physical therapist to give me all the details I didn't care about. "You'll also gain remarkable balance that'll not only help with a nice core, but you'll need it to walk down the aisle."

He snickered and let me know in his own little way that I was only doing this running thing to keep in the same shape I was in so I didn't go on one of those silly diets like most women I knew who had gotten engaged would do.

"All joking aside, using trails as an obstacle will make you stronger all over." He gave his last-ditch effort to get me to buy into this whole running thing before he darted off past me and the rest of the group to take his place back as the leader.

Instead of concentrating on my watch and how much longer we had until we came out on the other side of the trail, I decided to focus on my surroundings, which was no different than my volunteer position at the National Parks Committee, where it was my job to check out trails hikers would discover while they were visiting the Daniel Boone National Park.

Most of them turned out to be deer trails, the kind where deer would walk a path day in and out, making it appear as an actual mapped trail for hikers. It was those types of trails that would lead hikers to accidents or even untimely deaths.

The wind echoed from afar as it glided through the leaves of the big forest trees. On a regular walking hike, the breeze would've brought goose bumps with it and landed them along my skin. Not today. Nary a goose bump was going to show up on the stream of sweat going down my legs as the heat from the run pulsed through my veins.

The scurrying of squirrels caught my peripheral vision as they appeared to be desperately darting about to find nuts before the upcoming snow. It was fascinating how the animals in the forest knew when the seasons were changing, and I was lucky enough to be part of it.

We took a sharp curve of the trail. The forest and caverns were wide open where the leaves had fallen off the forest trees, making me very aware of the cliff drops on either side of me.

Stay on the path, I repeated in my head and tried not to get lost in the trickling sound of the creek down below. Though it was a dangerous stretch to hike, it was even more treacherous to run, and I wanted to eventually have everyone come to my wedding, not my funeral.

"What's wrong?" Christine turned around, jogging in place after she realized I wasn't running.

Granted, I was walking at a fast pace but not running.

"Are you okay?" A concerned look fell over her face as she jogged back toward me.

"I'm good. Just not going to make y'all come to a funeral instead of my wedding." I sounded like I was joking to her, but in reality, I wasn't comfortable jogging on a trail that I would deem to be difficult to hike much less run. "You go on ahead," I encouraged her. "I'll catch up."

"Are you sure?" she asked.

"I'll catch up at Red Barn." I made myself even more clear as to when I'd see her.

"If you're sure." She looked at me for some confirmation.

I gestured to her to go ahead, and she took off.

I walked even slower and kept my ears peeled, waiting for their feet pounding the rock-solid ground to move away from me before I sat down on a rotted log covered with green moss and a few fungi-style mushroom-looking creatures so I could not just catch my breath but take in the scenery.

This was what brought tourists to our little town and filled up the campground. The landscape of the Daniel Boone National Forest. Though I'd been calling this place home for a few years, there were still many trails of the over seven hundred thousand acres of land I'd yet to explore.

This was one of them.

Normally I stuck close to the trails located in downtown Normal, Happy Trails, or even the Old Train Station Motel, so I knew those fairly well, but not on this side of town, where the Cookie Crumble was located, which was more in the business district of town.

Christine had wanted to get closer to the hub of the tourists, but when she opened the Cookie Crumble, the building they were in now was the only one available at the time. I'd yet to see a business downtown go out of business or leave so it could make room for other shops, though I did keep my eyes peeled for anything that came through the park's office.

My heart returned to its normal beat, and my breathing steadied. There was no denying that the feeling I'd hear runners talk about—Christine called it the "runner's high"—was a thing.

I looked out over the cliff as I sat there, and a feeling of gratitude swept over me. This was something the scene alone would do to a person, but today, the feeling overtook me more than I'd expected.

A smile curled my lips. My heart felt so much lighter as the shadow from the sun passed over a part of the mountainous terrain, almost hiding the naked trees but lighting up the leaves that'd yet to fall where they'd make a color-quilted blanket on the trails for the runners to jog on.

Cracks, groans, and even a few limbs breaking told me I wasn't alone. The critters were very aware I was there. I let the sounds fill me up and kept my eyes closed. I put my hands down on the log and stretched my legs out to let the last bit of the sun beating down on this particular spot cover my face and warm it now that it was chilled from the dried sweat.

Mary Elizabeth popped into my head. I could hear her now. *"You're gonna catch the flu, running around in this cold weather with shorts and a T-shirt on."*

Even as a teen, on days like this, Mary Elizabeth would make me put on a sweater or a coat.

I opened my eyes and turned when I noticed a squirrel about two feet away had something in its mouth that didn't look like a nut.

He scurried off when I pulled my legs back in, dropping the object.

"I can't stand when people litter," I grumbled and pushed myself up to get the trash the squirrel had brought to my attention.

I'd learned you don't just pick up everything you see at first but to bend down and get a look at it to see if you need to use something between your hand and the object.

"Hmm," I hummed after I'd squatted down to take in the laminated photo with the tiny hole that had been ripped in the top. I flipped it over and noticed a small obituary had been placed behind the photo and realized it was one of those laminated cards the local funeral home passed out during a funeral service.

I also noticed the squirrel had stopped to see what I was going to do with it.

"Someone probably brought this guy's ashes out here and scattered them." I shook the small card at the squirrel. "Which you can't legally do."

I stood there, reading about the young man in the photo.

"Theodore Redford loved everything about nature. He loved to hike, kayak, swim, fish, and hunt. But his most enjoyable times were spent in the woods, hanging out with his best friends," I read out loud to the squirrel.

The little fuzzy-tailed creature stood up on his hind legs, his little hands crossed in front of him, and stared at me like he was really interested in Theodore's obituary.

"Theodore had a prodigious appetite that was always the highlight of any family meal or the Normal Diner, where there was a meal named in his honor." This piqued my interest, since I loved eating at the Normal Diner and couldn't wait to find out from Ty Randal just who this Theodore was. "Theodore was a kind man with a tender heart who always enjoyed connecting with people and who touched a lot of people's lives through his kind, unassuming nature." My voice trailed off. I turned the card back around to look at his photo then flipped it back over to see that Theodore's life was not long. Just seventeen years old when he died. "Was he your friend?" I asked the squirrel.

The squirrel had lost interest in me and darted down the trail, where I watched him almost take a dive off the trail and down the cliff. Something shimmered, catching my eye.

I walked over and bent down, carefully moving the fallen leaves out of the way to uncover what was glittering.

"A cross." I uncovered the small wooden cross that was buried into the ground. There was a metal thumbtack where the two pieces of sticks met to make the cross. "I bet you went right here."

I held the laminated photo up to the thumbtack, knowing the hole in the top of the photo was an exact match. The cross was buried far enough that it wasn't going to come out of the ground without a little tugging, so I plucked off the thumbtack and made a new hole in the photo with it before I pushed it back in place.

The runner's high I'd been feeling had quickly gone away when I realized this was probably the spot where the young man had died. There were a lot of these makeshift markers placed by family and friends when their loved ones succumbed to the treacherous dangers of the forest.

The forest was a gorgeous place to come and visit but would take you out in a literal heartbeat if you didn't respect it.

"Theodore Redford." I whispered his name to remember so I could look up this young man who'd died not too long before I'd moved to town.

A chilly breeze swept along the trail, rattling a few dried leaves in its path before it landed on my legs, where the goose bumps let me know they'd arrived.

CHAPTER THREE

"You didn't finish the trail run?" Christine Watson held a small highball glass in her hand, sucking the clear liquid through a straw.

"Actually, I sat down to take in the gorgeous views because you and I both know while running on a trail, you have to be careful and not fall off those cliffs." I stood at one of the tables near the stage, where the owners had cleared a few sit-down tables so people could stand while listening to the local band, Blue Ethel and the Adolescent Farm Boys.

Plus they knew tonight was going to be packed due to the fact it was the night everyone who came into town for Thanksgiving week was going to be here for the annual reunion.

"I don't know why y'all'd want to do something like that to yourself." Dottie Swaggert's nose curled in disgust. "You could at least smile every once in a while like you were enjoying it. Next time you see someone running"—she wagged her finger at us—"I want you to take a good hard look at them. Are they smiling?" Her head shook side to side, her lips turned down. The lines around them from her years of smoking deepened. "They look missssserable." Her southern twang made the already-long word twice as long.

"She's right, ya know." Abby elbowed me. She had the same drink as Christine, and the only reason I knew was because they had the same festive sprig of thyme along with an apple slice as a garnish. "Look at your brother." She threw a chin. "He acts like he went to school with all of Joel's friends."

Bobby Ray was right up in the middle of Joel Grassel and a bunch of his high school friends as they threw darts in what looked to be a heated game with all the hooting and hollering they were doing.

"I'm glad he's enjoying himself." I was going to bring up the photo of Theodore to Christine, but she'd walked off when she recognized someone from the past.

Through the crowd and now the turned-down overhead lights, I could see she and the man were having an intense conversation.

But my attention was quickly diverted when Hank Sharp walked into the restaurant. It was like my heart and his heart had a string connected. Our eyes met from far across the restaurant.

Both of us smiled at the same time. Mine faltered when Ellis Sharp, Hank's sister, walked up behind him.

"What on God's green earth is she doing with him?" Dottie asked in a nasty tone, which was what I felt when I saw Ellis.

It was like the spotlight had turned and shone right on the tall blond bombshell. I swear all the men on the dance floor, near the dartboard and the pool tables, all took off like a bat out of hell to get to her side.

"At least she'll be too busy with the men to put her nose into my business." I grabbed Abby's drink from her hands and took a big gulp. "Say, this is really good."

"It's an Autumn Fizz just for tonight's special." Abby wiggled her brows. "I'll go get us another one."

"Make it three!" Dottie held up three fingers, surprising me. "What? I like to tie one on every now and then. And tonight it looks like we are gonna need to tie on a few."

I pinched a smile and looked across the barn at the transformation. It was an old working barn with stalls, hayloft, and all the livestock before it was brought back to live as a fancy restaurant that could turn into a honky-tonk on a dime.

Long gone were the old stalls, haylofts, and dirt floor. The inside was completely open with exposed wooden beams. Each ceiling beam had strands of small round light bulbs, which were bright enough so you could see what you were eating but were dimmed to induce the feeling that you were under the moon. Soon they'd turn the restaurant into the most romantic place to eat for the winter by hanging snowflakes from the ceiling and placing several small Christmas trees around, but for tonight, the white tablecloth linens and little candlelight lantern centerpieces were stored and replaced with bluegrass music, loud chatter, flying darts, and flying beer bottles.

"Someone is gonna pay." Dottie jerked around when a beer bottle whizzed by her head. "If that had hit me, I'd be all up in someone's craw right now." She stomped just as another one smashed against the wall closest to us.

Screaming ensued, and a rumble like I'd never seen before stumbled right in front of our table, clearing the dance floor and causing Ethel Biddle to stop singing. The band's instruments faded but not Otis Gullett. He was so into his fiddling, he'd not recognized the pile of men had taken the spotlight off his fiddle playing.

Otis didn't even skip a string with his bow. He was a-gettin' it, and by the way the crowd was cheering on the wrestle mania, Otis had to've thought they were having a good time due to his fiddle playing until Ethel Biddle pushed him off the stage when the two men's bodies were flung up on the stage.

It was a little too close for comfort for me and the rest of the gals.

"Leave them!" I hollered at Dottie when I turned to her gathering up all the cocktail glasses from our table. "Leave them!"

I ran back to get her just as Hank came out of nowhere and lifted her up in the air, cradling her in his arms. It was like one of those hunky firefighter movies where he sweeps the woman off her feet in order to save her from a raging fire. The kind where the woman's hair was long and flowing and her lipstick was perfectly in the lines and not a smudge of makeup out of place even though there was a raging inferno behind her.

In this case, Dottie was crying. She had a death grip around Hank's neck. The edges of her hot-red hair were standing on end, the mascara streamed down her face, her red lipstick was smudged all around her lips and had reached her chin and the unlit cigarette stuck between her teeth.

Hank. He still looked good even with Dottie hanging off him.

"My oh my." Dottie tried to get herself together after Hank put her down outside in the parking lot of the Red Barn. "If I was May-bell-ine, I'd done dragged you down the aisle and never let you leave that camper." She wiggled her brows.

Even in the dark I could see Hank's face redden.

"You are one fine specimen." Dottie ran her fingernail down his bicep, though it was completely covered in his plaid shirt.

"That's enough." I moved Dottie in the stream of the parking lot lights to get a look at her. "Are you all right?"

"Fine as Otis's fiddle playin'." Her face was turned to Hank. She made kissy faces at him.

I took my fingers and moved her jaw to face me.

"What? He knows I'm teasin'. But I ain't teasin' you." She wagged her finger at me. "You need to get that man down the aisle, or someone is gonna sweep him out from under you."

"I think we are fine," I assured her though I did see he was talking to Natalie Willowby, a former citizen of Normal who was probably in town for the Red Barn Restaurant annual reunion.

"Are you now?" Dottie's sarcastic tone didn't go unnoticed, but luckily, my facial expression was because Abby and Bobby Ray came running over to make sure we were okay. "Did you see them almost whack me with a beer bottle?"

I knew I had some time to meander over Hank's way because Dottie would be telling this story for months if not years to come. I could hear her now talking about how two drunk men ruined the Red Barn Restaurant's annual informal citizen reunion.

"Oh, Hanky Panky, you looked like a hero carrying someone from a burning fire," I heard Natalie tell Hank. I rolled my eyes so hard I swore I could see my brains.

"You must've seen the same movie I did because I said that exact same thing." I made sure I placed my hand, engagement ring shining, flat on his chest. "I'm a lucky gal."

"Mmhmm," Natalie's hum came from deep inside because her lips were pinched tight.

"There you are." Ellis nearly fell into the middle of the group with a bottle of wine in her hands. "I mean, we almost died in there."

Ellis was good at stretching the truth of many things. This being one of those.

"Did you see Hanky Panky's ring he gave to my soon-to-be sister-in-law who has yet to nail down a date for my poor brother?" Ellis was drunk.

She threw her arm around my neck, and the wine bottle tipped over, pouring down not only on Hank but also me.

"Whooopsie." She cackled, removing her arm from around me and throwing her hand up to cover her smiling mouth.

Even drunk Ellis looked pretty. She stood a little taller than me. Just enough so that certain clothes looked frumpy on me, but anything she wore looked as though it was tailored especially for her.

She positioned one arm across herself with the wine bottle dangling from her hand. Her rosy complexion was perfect for her job as a model, but the drunk rosy complexion was really pretty too.

She wore a smirk on her face that fit her attitude. Her thin shape was accentuated under the tight black pants and tight black turtleneck, which made her features even more striking. Her blond hair was straight and loose. It was a great style for tossing, which she did with every gesture she made.

"I heard. Congratulations." Natalie, though she didn't mean it, did seem a little embarrassed for Ellis. She took a quick look at my hand that was now at my side before she realized I'd seen her. "Can I see?" She put her hand out.

"It was my granny Agnes's." Hank's voice was so tender and loving. He put a hand on the small of my back and used the other to wipe down his shirt where Ellis had spilled the wine.

"Oh, Hanky Panky." Ellis continued to use his childhood nickname. The one he didn't like but with Ellis he tolerated it. "I'm so sorry. I hope you can get that out of your plaid shirt." She snickered.

Ellis and I had our differences but had put those behind us. But when it came to Natalie, Ellis had tried her hardest to break us up and set them up. I wasn't sure how it had all gone down, but when Hank and I had broken up, there'd been some rumors of him and Natalie going on a few dates. I wasn't sure how accurate the gossip was due to the fact Hank had moved away from Normal and Natalie had also left to take a coroner's job, since she was the assistant coroner to Colonel Holz.

"It's very pretty." She dropped my hand and pushed her hands into the pockets of her jeans. "I bet Agnes was very happy."

Though I wanted to think Natalie wasn't being sincere, she was, or at least she appeared to be, and then I knew she was because one of the rowdy men came over with his rhinestone button-down shirts tucked into skintight jeans with a huge belt buckle and a set of cowboy boots on him that he'd no way gotten here in Normal.

"Hank, man, how the hell are ya?" He swung an arm around Natalie before he slammed a hand slap on Hank's arm. He dragged the sleeve of his shirt across his bloody lip and smiled like a big dufus.

"I'm good, Garrett." Hank gave a half smile. Immediately I could tell he didn't care for the guy.

That was when I found myself not listening to anything they said because my crazy mind went directly to wondering if Hank was a wee bit jealous this guy had his arm around Natalie.

Ahem, I cleared my throat.

"I'm sorry. Man." Hank did the guy lingo. "I'm rude. This is my fiancée, Mae."

"Weeeedoggie, you got you a good one." Garrett winked at me from underneath the cowboy hat, making the air around us a little more nippy than it really was.

Flashing lights lit up the darkness that'd covered the night sky. They were quickly followed by the sirens.

"Looks like they done went and called the law." Garrett snuggled Natalie closer to him and gave her a kiss on top of her head. "Now don't you worry about me. I'll go talk to the sheriff, and I'll see you back at the bed-and-breakfast."

"I'll wait." Natalie grabbed ahold of him, fearful like, a side of her I'd never seen.

"Suit yourself." Garrett snickered and looked at me and Hank. "If Mitchell Redford don't stop runnin' that mouth of his, we'll be doing this again tomorrow night." Garrett pointed his finger at the restaurant and moseyed over to Al Hemmer's sheriff's truck.

"So you and Garrett Callis?" Hank shuffled his foot. "How did that happen?"

"I was out to dinner one night, and who would walk in but Garrett. You know when you're in a new town and see someone familiar, it's kinda nice." Natalie told her story to Hank while I gawked at Garrett dramatically explaining to Al his side of the brawl. "Strange because you know I love all of nature."

I had no idea where she was going with this.

"Naturally since I grew up here, but Garrett's mom has this amazing greenhouse. A couple in fact. They're crazy big, and I never knew about it." She laughed, dragged her empty ring finger up to the necklace around her neck and fiddled with it in a flirty way.

I curled my hand around Hank's elbow. Her eyes took in my movement. They moved up to my face, and she pinched a grin.

"Anyways, we've spent the past couple of days helping her water, fertilize, and prune the plants she has in there while they are out of town for the holidays. It's amazing really." Her hand fell from the chain, and she clasped them in front of her. "You know, Mae, I was telling Garrett about the Milkery, and I think Mary Elizabeth would love to have some of his mom's products to sell."

"Is that right?" My face stilled as I gave her a blank stare. She stiffened at my response.

"Maybe—" Hank leaned back and smiled at me. "We can ask her at Thanksgiving. But she might already have someone for the upcoming spring. You know businesses plan things like those months ahead of time. Mary Elizabeth, well, she's always a season ahead." Hank gave a nervous ramble.

"He's the one who should be arrested! He killed my cousin!" One of the sheriff's deputies had dragged out the other guy, who I was assuming to be Mitchell Redford.

I shifted my gaze to Christine Watson, Will Denning, and a few of the other runners from the running group, who were also standing in a circle, watching what was going on.

"I have no idea what that was all about in there. One minute we were dancing and enjoying talking to everyone, then out of nowhere, Mitchell Redford and Harrison Pierce started making trouble." Natalie threw an eye over to the sheriff, where two other men stood next to Al Hemmer and Garrett.

All three men looked heated, and Al was trying to keep the peace by putting his hand up between them, but when they started throwing punches, not only was Al's hand knocked out of the way, Al was pummeled by Garrett's fist.

"Garrett!" Natalie screamed and ran over to him, but she didn't get there fast enough.

The deputies cuffed him and threw him in the back of one of their sheriff's cars.

Natalie beat on the window. "I'll come down there! No! I'm coming!" she hollered after the car as it took off with the swirling lights and whirling siren. "Here! Here's your phone!"

She held the cell phone up in the air as she tried to break through the police barricade, but she didn't make it in time.

"Maybe that'll whack some sense into Al." Dottie was serious.

"Go help her." I flung a finger at Natalie and instructed Hank.

"Why me?" He gave me an awkward look.

"Because that's what you do." I gave him a little shove to get him moving. Reluctantly, he wandered over as Dottie darted straight toward me.

"What on earth is he doing?" Dottie took a draw off her cigarette. The tip lit up like the butt end of a lightning bug.

"You said he was a hero. He's going to be a hero." I smiled when I saw Natalie melt into his chest.

"Not her hero, May-bell-ine." Dottie's words hit me as the clouds in the fall night sky parted, the moon peeking out and its beam spot-lighting the look on Natalie's face.

A look I'd recognized from the many times she'd tried to get her sweet southern claws into my Hanky Panky.

There was a lot of huh, umms, and elbowing from Dottie through the pack of cigarettes she'd gone through while we stood there waiting for Hank. Only he wasn't alone.

"Natalie's purse is in Garrett's car, and she can't get into her parent's house without her keys," Hank was explaining to me with kid gloves on.

"I need my keys." Natalie's jaw clenched as she interrupted Hank. "Hank is the only person I know who can jimmy a car door to unlock it. The sheriff deputies said they don't have those tools, and no one has a hanger. Not even in the restaurant."

"Not a wire hanger. They have others." Hank continued to explain further to me when he honestly just needed to cut to the chase. "I have some back at the camper."

"That solves it." Dottie threw her cigarette on the ground and snuffed it out. "Let's go home. See ya next time you're in town, Natalie."

"You can't leave me here. I have no ride," Natalie whined. "Hank said he'd go get a hanger."

"Yes." This time he stopped her from talking and turned his attention directly to me. "You and Dottie can follow me and Natalie back to the campground. I'll grab a hanger and bring her back here to unlock it then give her a ride back to her parents."

"There will be no such doings." Dottie wagged her finger in Hank's face. "Me and Natalie will sit right here while you and May-bell-ine drive to the campground to get the hanger."

"You don't need to do that. We can all go." Natalie's eyes narrowed. "Come on, Hank. I'll ride with you just like we planned."

"I think Dottie's plan is great." I grabbed Hank by the hand and pulled him toward his car, even though I had driven me and Dottie here. "We will be back in a flash."

"I'll go with you," Natalie called after us.

"No, you won't either. You'll stay right here with me."

I overheard Dottie and couldn't help but snicker.

There was so much tension in the car when Hank and I had driven back to the campground, it was almost hard to breathe.

"Fine. I'll go first. Why are you mad?" I asked Hank, thankful the darkness had covered us and he couldn't see my set jawline.

"I'm not mad. I guess I'm confused." Though I couldn't see him, I could hear him suck in a deep breath.

"Confused?" I asked.

"You don't want me to talk to Natalie, then you want me to rescue her. It's confusing what you want me to do and not be mad at me." He laughed. "I can't win."

"I know it's confusing, and it's conflicting to me too." I reached over and grabbed his hand that was resting on his thigh. "But I have the ring and the man, so I don't mind you helping her anymore. She's a trigger to how she treated me and the underhanded things she did when you weren't my fiancé." I said it in a teasing way.

"I love you and only you, so if you want me to help her, I will. But other than that, she never crosses my mind." Hank turned into the campground.

The small posts with the solar-powered lights dimly lit up the drive leading up to the campground, where several campfires glowed from the hot embers with occupied chairs around the fire rings.

It was a funny thing in a campground. Everything started and came to life around 7:00 p.m. due to the nature of the sun having long set and the darkness filling in the space. Also around then, the campers would've gotten in from any sort of hiking or day activities and gotten their grills fired up or coals lit.

Everyone was respectful of everyone else. I rolled down the truck window and gestured for Hank to drive the long way around so I could check on everyone.

There were a few of our guests intermingling, which was the most special part for me. It was times like this when they gathered to learn about each other and share information or knowledge they might have about camping or even discussing different campgrounds they'd visited around the many national parks in the states.

There was different music coming from a few different sites. One of the campers had their radio on and was sitting around their fire with some holiday beverages when the next camper had a man strumming on his guitar and a woman playing a harmonica.

"I wish we'd just stayed here tonight," Hank said and looked over at me. "This is our party right here."

"Yeah," I agreed. "I do miss it when we aren't here."

"Maybe we should get married here. I mean, look at that." Hank's headlights flashed on the backdrop of the Daniel Boone National Forest. "I know we can't see the colors right now in the dark, but can you imagine what kind of photo that'd be?"

"Just when I didn't think I could love you anymore." I used my hand to extend the seat belt across my shoulder and leaned over to kiss him. "I think you've had a great idea."

He parked the truck but kept it running in front of his camper when we got around the campground. I sat there waiting for him and thought about a campground wedding.

"Who on earth would've thought I'd have my wedding at a campground?" I talked to myself with a giggle. Then I thought about Mary Elizabeth.

Lordy help me.

Hank hurried out of the fifth wheel with a wire hanger in his hand.

"What's with the smile?" Hank asked when the overhead light in the truck illuminated. He put the hanger on the floorboard in the second seat of the truck and got his seat belt on.

"You make me happy." I shrugged and knew no matter how much he helped Natalie tonight, I had nothing to worry about.

One problem with that thinking... I'd not thought about what the rest of the week would bring.

CHAPTER FOUR

"You dropped her off at the Milkery?" Christine Watson asked on our early-morning jog. "I mean, I saw her get in the car with you and Hank last night, but I figured you were taking her down to the station to get Garrett out of jail."

"Nope." I couldn't believe the energy I had this morning. I would love to have thought it was the runner's high, but this was purely me getting my deep-rooted anger out about Natalie using last night's situation to get Hank to go above and beyond the hero status I wanted him to play. "Garrett had told her to go to the Milkery, where they are staying. And Mary Elizabeth didn't even tell me Natalie was staying there."

Christine and I had stayed up way past our bedtime to think about running with her usual morning running group. Or she was just being nice and agreed to run with me later in the morning, leaving the other runners to their usual early schedule.

They weren't about to skip a day of training for the Turkey Trot this weekend, but I was hoping for a much easier run this morning, since today was Thanksgiving, and I would be feasting on some delicious Mary Elizabeth turkey with all the fixings.

"But she seemed pretty upset after Garrett was taken to jail." I was so glad we stayed on the road even though we had to keep our eyes out for the heavier-than-usual traffic on the rural roads leading into downtown.

I noticed Christine's sudden silence.

"Do you know something about Garrett?" I wanted to know all I could about Natalie and what appeared to be her boyfriend. At first she was all into him and upset when he was put in the deputies' car after he slugged Al.

I was figuring the fist to Al's little jaw wasn't meant for Al, but all the same, it wasn't good to hit the sheriff even if the sheriff was Al Hemmer.

"He's been gone for a long time from Normal, so I really don't know him." Christine talked as if we were sitting on a porch swing, having us a social conversation, not running at a faster clip than I'd prefer. But she was giving me all the details about Garrett, which tied to Natalie, who I didn't want any part of her woman claws in *my* Hanky Panky.

"He used to run around with a crowd of my friends. I'll say that I hope he's grown up a lot." Notice she didn't say a little, telling me in no uncertain terms Garrett Callis was a hell-raiser back in the day.

"That's certainly someone I didn't see Natalie with," she finished as we rounded the big curve before the Red Barn Restaurant off in the distance. "That tells me I need to give him the benefit of the doubt and believe he's grown up."

The sun started to inch up over the mountain, reminding me of one of those push-up sherbet pops with the plastic stick, but if you pushed too hard, the whole cardboard cylinder container of sherbet would pop up. That was how the sun was. Once it peeked, it popped.

It was shining brightly, giving light to the activity going on in the parking lot of the restaurant.

"Are they hosting some sort of free Thanksgiving dinner?" Christine asked when she too noticed the flurry of activity.

"I think that's a great idea, but I don't think the sheriff would be there or some deputies or even Tucker Pyle's ranger truck if that was the case." I felt my legs pick up speed, almost sprinting toward the parking lot to get a look. "Besides—" My breathing heaved out of my chest, causing my words to come out exhausted. "Coke Ogden is hosting a free Thanksgiving supper to anyone who wants to come in the barn."

The Old Train Station Motel had an events venue on the property. Since Coke didn't have much family left, she was always hosting various things for the community so people weren't left out during anything, including holidays.

"Will and the running group are there," she pointed out and darted off, leaving me far behind.

The closer I got to the restaurant, the less focus I had on the ripening, vivid colors of red and orange of the mountain landscape that kept me going on my runs, turning instead to the yellow caution tape strung around the side of the restaurant like the twinkling lights on all the campers at Happy Trails Campground.

I mean, it was hanging all over the place.

My feet ached with each stride as it got bigger and bigger. The ache in my side got stronger and stronger until I finally noticed Colonel Holz's hearse.

"This ain't good." I had slowed when the sudden realization someone was dead had pushed any sort of running right on out of my mind. Then it hit me even harder. It was like throwing kerosene on a fire. My adrenaline exploded, and I took off. Before I knew it, I was next to the running group, albeit bent over with my hands gripping my knees and sucking in air as though it were through a straw, but I was there.

"What—" I sucked in a breath. "Happened?" I let go of the breath, standing up and taking another deep inhale.

Christine turned around. Her eyes were already red around the edges, and I noticed she was in a shocked, upset emotional stage.

"Christine?" I put a hand on her. "Who is it?"

"I can't believe it." The words coming out of her mouth matched the look on her face. "It's Mitchell Redford. The guy Garrett got into a fight with last night." She gulped.

"I'm sorry. Did you know him?" I asked, not sure whether to grab her in a huge hug or just let her be sad due to the nature of the shock we'd run up on.

"Know him?" Will peered over Christine's head and looked at me. "She dated him for like three years."

"Five," she corrected him in a whisper before she buried her head into my shoulder. "Five years."

"I'm so sorry." I patted her on the back with both arms around her. I tried to get a better look at the scene to see what happened, but Al had it pretty well cornered off and a sheet hung up. "How do you know it's Mitchell?"

"Colonel told us." Will had his hands planted on his waist like the rest of the running group. They weren't standing still like me and Christine. Some had their arms up over the heads, stretching them out, knees bent back as they stood on one leg as if they were stretching out their muscles. But their eyes were fixated on the unfolding situation.

"Did you talk to him last night?" I asked her, remembering her walking off to go talk to a guy last night, but I'd not gotten who it was until it clicked that this might be him.

She did look awfully giddy and happy to be talking to him.

"I talked to him for a long time last night." She pulled away from me and wiped the tears off her face. "In fact, it was right before Garrett Callis started the fight."

The car. My jaw dropped. My head turned, and I knew I recognized the car, though it was in the daylight.

"What? You know something." Christine's nostrils flared. There seemed to be some anger coming out. "Tell me what you know. I know you and how you always kinda know things," she demanded.

"Last night when Garrett was arrested, his car keys were in his pants pocket. Natalie couldn't get in the car to get her purse where her parent's house keys were to get in their house even though I'm guessing she could've woken them up, but regardless, Hank had to come to her rescue and get the car door open." I left out the details of us having to go to the campground to grab a coat hanger in order for Hank to get the car doors unlocked. It was beside the point. "That's the car."

"We are going to take off now," Will interrupted us. "Are you going to be okay?"

"I'll take care of her." There was no need for anyone else to stay with Christine. I'd call Hank, and he could come to my rescue this morning. "We will get a ride home. I don't think she needs to be running."

"Yeah. Y'all go on." She looked at him and the group. All of them had very concerned looks on their faces for their friend. "Mae is here."

"Okay. I hope to see you in the morning?" He said it as more of a question than a statement before he darted off.

"Mae." She said my name in a way that really got my attention.

"Yeah?" I looked at her.

"Do you think Garrett had something to do with Mitchell's death?" she asked.

"Why would you say that?" I wondered if she knew something I didn't.

And she did.

Sorta.

"When we were kids, Mitchell's cousin Ted was on a hike with us, and he fell to his death." I blinked back into my memory of the hike from yesterday.

"Wait. Theodore Redford?" She nodded. "The one who loved nature and"—I spouted out all the stuff I recalled from the obituary card—"the trail we were on yesterday?"

She nodded again.

"I was thinking about him the entire time but didn't say anything because it was too sad to think about." Both of us watched a little movement from behind the sheet Al had hung up, but there wasn't anything to be seen. When the sheet swayed a little, it drew our attention. "Mitchell always said Garrett pushed Ted off the trail to his death because they were arguing, and both were hotheaded. Of course we'd been drinking, so I never in a million years thought it was true, but last night and now..." Her voice trailed off, giving way to silent tears.

Colonel Holz walked out from behind the sheet just as my phone chirped a text. I unzipped the fanny pack I wore when I went on these jogs and took my phone out. It was Dottie texting the Laundry Club Ladies group message that there'd been a murder at the Red Barn Restaurant.

Murder? I thought to myself so as not to get Christine upset anymore.

"Colonel is getting the gurney. Do you think he'll let me see Mitchell?"

Another text chirped in from Betts, saying someone from the church had called Lester. Though Lester wasn't a preacher of the Normal Baptist Church any longer and had been pardoned of his jail sentence, people here tended to overlook things. But in Lester's case, I could only imagine it was for the fact the man wasn't going to live much longer, and though he did the crime, he was still the man they loved and in some weird way found comfort in him.

Queenie shot back a text asking if we knew who it was, to which Abby responded she'd heard it was Garrett Callis, to which I replied with the correct name, Mitchell Redford, then took a quick photo of the Red Barn Restaurant sign minus the crime scene to prove I was there.

Then my phone rang, and it was Dottie. She wanted all the details. I was sure of it.

I sent her to voicemail, saying I couldn't talk and would be home shortly. Then she sent me back a text that read she needed to talk to me now right before my phone rang.

"Shortly better be soon. Natalie Willowby just drove past the office. I'm watching her pull up to Hank's camper as we speak, and he's sitting outside." Dottie grunted. I knew she was getting a better angle to see out the office window. She would know Natalie's car, since Hank had been keeping his camper there, living in it even while we were broken up.

"He's just offered her his cup of coffee. Oh. She took it." A shameful gasp expelled from her and through the phone.

There was silence.

"What, Dottie?" I found myself suddenly thrown into her shenanigans.

"They went inside." The excited tone in her voice took a shift. Almost sounded as if she were sad for me.

"We got murder, huh?" Waldo Willy snuck up behind me. I swear he did. He snuck. If I'd seen him coming, I would've stopped him from talking since Christine was standing there, and she didn't yet know the particulars of Mitchell's death.

"Is that Waldo?" Dottie's tone shifted right back up and pierced my ear.

"Dottie, I've got to go." I wanted to hurry off the phone. The quicker I got Christine out of here, the faster I could get back to the campground and see what was really going on inside of Hank's camper. "I'll be back shortly," I said again.

"Murder?" Christine's shoulders slumped. "Mitchell was murdered." As she looked at me for some sort of confirmation, I watched as her eyes clouded with a hazy sadness.

"I don't know." I put a hand on her forearm. "Waldo doesn't know." I gave Waldo the wonky eye, but he didn't get the point that I wanted him to shush.

"You knew him?" Waldo had no couth about him. "How did you know him?"

"Honestly." I stomped a foot and pointed to Christine when she ran off toward Colonel, no doubt wanting some answers to Waldo's claim.

"What is that, the girlfriend? From my research, he didn't have a girlfriend." Waldo flipped the pages of his notebook.

"Did your research tell you he had friends? Good friends, and she is —was—one of them. Or did your research tell you to have a little more compassion?" I shook my head and headed after my friend, even though I was sure I was taking out my frustrations with the fact my fiancé was having coffee with a woman who didn't give two cares in the world if her so-called boyfriend had killed someone.

"How was I to know she was his girlfriend?" he asked and kept his eye on the fluid situation.

"She's not his girlfriend anymore. I mean, for a long time but in high school or something. Don't quote me. I don't know all the details." I sighed and tried to make out what Christine and Colonel were saying to one another.

By the way Colonel was shaking his head and her face jutted up in his, she wasn't getting what she wanted, and that was to see the body.

"Why do you say it was murder?" I asked him.

"Came through on the police scanner." It wouldn't surprise me if Waldo kept the scanner running all day and all night. "I don't know how, but the sheriff's deputy who called it in said the runners found a dead body. When the deputy came, he called dispatch for backup so they could look around the area because he said it appeared to be a murder."

Hearing what Waldo had said, it was making sense with all the deputies scouring the scene in the surrounding area, probably looking for evidence. Then there was the door of the Red Barn Restaurant propped open, that I'd not noticed until now. There was literally nothing we could do here or help in any way. Al seemed to have it all under control, and he didn't even give me another glance to ask any questions.

"It was good seeing you, Waldo. Have a happy Thanksgiving." It took everything in me not to invite him to the Milkery for Thanksgiving supper tonight, but in light of what was happening before our eyes, I imagined he would be knee-deep in old newspaper articles and online research to find out anything and everything about Mitchell.

Plus it was Thanksgiving. Not a time to discuss murders and those things.

After I excused myself politely from Waldo, I walked over to Christine.

"What did Colonel say?" I asked in hopes my assumptions were wrong.

Waldo walked past us and took his own shot at getting some information from one of the sheriff's deputies.

"He couldn't confirm or deny who it is or how they died. He simply said there was a body." The look of despair had taken her vibrant glow from the run completely away. "I asked if it was a man or woman. He wouldn't even comment on it. I told him if they thought it was Mitchell, I could identify him."

"Why don't we leave, and I'll see what Hank can find out." I offered a sympathetic smile. "I'll call him to come get us."

A few quick head nods and another swipe of her hand underneath her running nose, she agreed, and I dialed Hank's number.

I was sent straight to voicemail. I redialed. Same thing.

"Well, ladies, it appears the law is being tight-lipped." Waldo had sauntered on over. "But I have a good reason to believe it's…"

"Waldo," I interrupted him. "Can you drive us back to the Cookie Crumble? We don't feel like running, especially if a killer is on the loose."

"A killer?" he questioned.

"I don't know. I mean, the governor did pardon a lot of people over the last few months, and a few of them were in the clink for killing people." I shrugged in hopes it would spark an interest for him to go down the rabbit hole of checking out the prisoners who had been released. "Sometimes they get a little restless. Antsy. Fall back into their old ways."

"That's good." He bit his lower lip and shook his ink pen at me. "Yeah. They aren't going to tell me anything here. I don't even think they know. I'll get a little research done today and then hopefully later get some detailed information about the murder."

"Stop saying that," Christine spit out. The stages of grief were starting to show, and the angry side of her was coming out. "If—and I say if—it's Mitchell and he was murdered, they are going to pay."

She left us standing there as she stomped toward Waldo's car.

"Oh, it's Mitchell, and he was murdered." Waldo's words sent a terrifying chill to my heart.

CHAPTER FIVE

"Be back shortly?" Dottie's brow ticked up. She stood in the grass between the campground's driveway and the lake, watching Fifi run around chasing the ducks back into the cold water of the lake. "Shortly doesn't mean an hour later." She slid her gaze past me, over my shoulder, to where Natalie's car was still parked on the concrete pad in front of Hank's fifth wheel.

"I'm confident in my relationship that nothing is going on." I had a sick feeling that I was trying to convince myself when in reality, the look in Natalie's eyes when she stared at Hank last night told me no matter how many Garrett Callises were in her life, she'd still have that one little piece in her heart for Hank.

"Then why does she need to come see him on Thanksgiving? And why has she been in there for over an hour?" Dottie pulled out her cigarette case and batted out one of her smokes.

"I don't know, but I've got to get the corn pudding made and get showered and ready before we head over to the Milkery." I looked around the campground and saw some campers coming to life.

Before they'd all checked in, I'd given them the flyer from Coke Ogden about the communal Thanksgiving dinner she was hosting at the Old Train Station Motel so they knew they had a place to go for

Thanksgiving if they didn't already have plans. But now I was more grateful than ever Coke did plan this because a lot of people made reservations to eat at the Red Barn Restaurant.

Only today it would've been turned into the white-tableclothed, fancy-eating place it generally was since last night was a special and traditional occasion for the locals. Now that it was a murder scene, or at least the rumblings of one, there was no way it would be cleared for them to open, leaving everyone out of a place to have their Thanksgiving meal.

"She must've seen you coming home." Dottie pointed the lit cigarette at Natalie. She'd emerged from Hank's camper. She gave us a slight wave. "Hey there! Happy Thanksgiving."

Shocked, I looked at Dottie, my upper lip ticked up in the corner.

"What?" Dottie asked with a smile on her face and a wave of her hand. "Gotta be nice to girls like her. She thinks she's so fancy and all, but the only culture that woman will ever have is a yeast infection."

I snorted and smiled.

"See. I made you smile. Now wave like it's no big deal she's been alone with your man for an hour." Dottie was good at making me laugh, and I did what she said.

To say Natalie was taken back by the smiles and waves was an understatement. When she smiled back at us, I could see the nervous quiver on her lips.

Nervous. Just the way I liked her.

I heard Hank tell her goodbye and he'd be in touch. Like the southern gentleman he was, he'd opened her car door and then shut it once she was in.

"I wish she'd shut that on her foot. Not enough to break it but just hurt it a bit." Dottie sucked on the cigarette and then let it go in a steady stream in front of her.

"We can't always get what we wish for." I sighed since there Natalie was, in my face, in my campground when I'd wished many, many times that she'd leave Normal.

Which she did. But here she was again. I should've added to my wish that she'd stay gone.

"Good for her that I'm in the holiday spirit of joy and love that I don't have any issue with her." I clicked my tongue for Fifi to come and leave the ducks alone. "I'll pick you up at four."

"Then you better get to baking the corn puddin'. It takes a while." She and I both looked back to the top of the campground when we heard another set of tires coming up the drive to Natalie's tires leaving.

It was Henry Bryant, my handyman.

"What is he doing here?" I asked Dottie. An amused look covered my face, knowing good and well he was probably there to visit with her.

"He called and said his plans to go to the Red Barn Restaurant had been canceled, so I called up Mary Elizabeth and asked if she had room for one more." Dottie refused to give an inkling she had a little some-thing-something for Henry.

"Whatever you need to tell yourself to make you feel better about your feelings for him." I loved making her squirm when it came to the matter of her own heart.

"May-bell-ine." She tsked. "You've lost your mind."

"Oh, you can dish it, but you can't take it," I joked as she walked to the front of the campground to meet him.

"Take what?" Hank walked up with Chester, which only made Fifi and Chester run off, chasing the ducks together.

"Nothing." I looked up at him and melted into those big green eyes that stood out against his black head of hair. "What did Natalie want?"

"The guy Garrett had a fight with ended up dead. Garrett was released early this morning on his own recognizance, and the murder was placed an hour after he was released. Natalie said Al Hemmer came back to her parent's place looking for him when they went to the Milk-ery, and Mary Elizabeth said he asked her for a ride back to the Red Barn to get his car. His car is still there and now in sheriff's custody."

"What does this have to do with you?" I wasn't following what happened to Mitchell Redford had to do with Hank.

"Natalie says Garrett didn't do it," Hank said.

Did he know something I didn't? Was Waldo right?

"Didn't do what?" I questioned.

"Have anything to do with what happened to Mitchell." Hank's shoulders fell. "Natalie said when Al came by, they insinuated there was some foul play. They pulled some video this morning from the Red Barn's outside alarm camera, where it shows Garrett is there with Mitchell."

"Foul play?" I gulped. What exactly did Waldo know about this? He knew enough to be very confident in saying Mitchell was murdered. "Did Natalie say what Al thinks?"

"No. Al didn't tell her. Garrett. He's disappeared. She wants me to investigate it." Hank ran his hand through his hair. "I knew you weren't going to like it, but I told her I'd see what I could find out. Maybe Granny has some information."

"Yeah. Maybe." I wasn't about to touch all this with a ten-foot pole. "Fifi," I called. She jerked up from the edge of the lake and looked back at me. "Let's get a treat!"

Bribing the poor dog was the only way I could get her away from Chester. Chester also knew the word *treat*, so he also darted back to me.

"Want help?" The way he looked at me, it was too hard for me to say no.

"Of course. You can open the cans of cream corn." I kissed him, and we walked back to my camper. "I've been thinking about the wedding and who might be bridesmaids for me."

"Yeah." Hank smiled. "Let me guess, Betts, Abby, and Ellis?"

"Ellis?" My eyes shot open. Luckily, I was opening the camper door and wasn't looking at him.

I took the step up into the camper and walked over to the small pantry door.

"Aren't the sisters of the groom always in the wedding?" he asked.

"I don't know, but I was talking about Dottie." I took out a couple cans of corn and cream corn. I planted a smile on my face before I turned around. "But of course Ellis will be a bridesmaid." I gulped back the idea of her doing the worst thing you could do at a southern wedding, upstage the bride.

Ellis would definitely have her model face on, and the fact she was there would upstage me anyways, but in order to keep the peace, I would do whatever it took to make Hank happy.

"Wouldn't she be the maid of honor?" he asked.

"Dottie?" My voice rose an octave.

"No." He moved behind me, brushing his fingers along the small of my back. "Ellis."

He was in the cabinet underneath the sink, which told me he was getting the glass dish I needed for baking.

The lump in my throat that had Ellis's name on it was getting much harder for me to swallow.

"I've not thought that hard about it, but we can definitely talk. But I was talking about Dottie being a bridesmaid." I choked down the lump.

"Dottie?" he questioned. "She's a little old, don't you think? I mean, maybe she can keep the guest book or give out those little brochure thingies."

"Old?" I set the cans on the counter and reached for the jar of dog treats. "I didn't forget you two."

Fifi's toenails clicked on the floor as she danced in front of me. Chester's tongue was hanging out in anticipation. I handed them a treat each, and both ran to a different dog bed to eat them.

"Is there an age limit on being a bridesmaid?" I asked, a little baffled by his response.

"I don't know, Mae. I'm a guy, and the only weddings I've really been to are people who are young, I guess. I'm sorry. I think Dottie would make a great bridesmaid, though she might bedazzle her dress." He brought up a topic I would definitely have to address with her.

"Mary Elizabeth would die." I snickered at the thought. "But at least I'm at the stage of starting to think about things."

"What about a date?" he asked and took the can opener out of the drawer while I took out the dry ingredients from the pantry.

"Now you're pushing it," I teased and took out a recipe from my mama. My birth mama's. It was one of the few things that'd been saved from the fire, and it was in her own handwriting, which I cherished so much. "But I am leaning more toward next fall."

"We both love fall, and with Mary Elizabeth's planning style, I'm guessing she'll need that long to plan." Hank knew this would warm the cockles of Mary Elizabeth.

"You are a suck-up," I teased him and followed it up with a kiss before we both started to make the corn pudding, which wasn't really that hard or too uncommon. It was the history and the memories I held inside that made this so special.

I remembered her in our little kitchen's house where she made this on Thanksgiving. Mary Elizabeth had always been so good about it. She even insisted we make it every year even though she didn't like corn. She made sure it was part of our annual Thanksgiving dinner. When I was a little older, she started having me make it on my own. She'd tell everyone who came, because she'd always had a very open invitation to anyone who needed or wanted to come for the holidays, how it was my mama's special dish, and she'd tell everyone how proud of me she was that I'd made it.

Hank had embraced every single side of me. The good, the bad, and the ugly. Though I'd like to think the good outweighed the bad and ugly.

"What is your take on the whole Mitchell thing?" I asked Hank.

"I don't have much right now in the way of whether or not I'll help Natalie or Garrett because I don't have the facts of the case." Hank got us Coke while I put the corn pudding in the oven.

He sat down at the small café table for two that was the perfect size for my small campervan.

"I called Granny to see what they had, and she said she'd get back with me, that they were all running around like they had no idea what they were doing." He snickered and played with the lid of the candle, which was shaped like a pumpkin.

Holidays were one of my favorite times to decorate, and as soon as the first day of fall hit, I had decorated my campervan with all things

Halloween. I even took down my twinkling lights strung all over the inside of my campervan and replaced them with little pumpkin and bat lights. I'd changed the small area rugs out for ghost and goblins and even my bedcovers in my bedroom to sheets with fall leaves printed on them.

It didn't stop there. Once November hit, I'd switched all the Halloween items to fall items, more along the lines of pumpkins and leaves, though I did put the clear twinkly lights back up and all the Halloween things in storage. Even the soaps in the bathroom and kitchen sinks were switched out to fall scents in glittery pumpkin-shaped containers.

The holidays had a certain feel-good to them, and even though the holidays were sometimes tough due to the nature of my blood family, I knew my friends and Mary Elizabeth were family that I'd been able to choose and keep, making it a little easier to fill the void in my heart.

Now that I had Hank, and even though we weren't super close with his parents, I still felt a belonging of family.

"Did you know Christine Watson dated Mitchell back in the day?" I asked Hank.

"Are you having some sort of notion about snooping around?" Hank glared at me from across the table as I stood next to the small love seat to fold the blanket with the words *It's Fall Y'all* printed really big.

"No. It's just in my nature to think this way." I shrugged, laid the blanket over the right arm of the love seat since Chester had found a comfy spot, and snuggled up to the left side of the couch. "I guess when I found the memorial for Theodore Redford on the trail, it seems like it's all a strange coincidence."

Not that I was all woo-woo or anything, but it was like one of those times you'd hear about when you think of someone and literally the next day you see them or they call you. It was kinda like that. I saw the memorial because of a squirrel, and now his cousin ends up dead?

Again, coincidence?

"I didn't even think about that." The lines between Hank's eyes deepened. He picked up his Coke and took a drink. "You were on the trail?" Worry laced his words.

"The running group took it, and I had stopped. When I did, it was near the memorial for him. I'd not realized it was a memorial until I uncovered the small cross where the laminated burial card had been held there with a small nail." I tidied up all the junk I'd put in the two captain's chairs that were turned around to make more seating in the campervan.

Things like Fifi's leash, which went into a basket near the chairs, my purse, and the week-old junk mail that needed to go in the garbage can. Things haphazardly thrown around, that even surprised me since I was really a clean freak and kept things picked up. Lately I'd found myself spending more and more time outside due to the nature of the lower temperatures, making it hard for me not to explore more.

"I fixed the card back on the cross and didn't even think about it until today when Christine and I ran on our own." Satisfied with the results of my quick pick up, I sat down at the table across from Hank, but he stood up.

"Well, it was a hard time when all that happened. Mitchell actually blamed Garrett for all of it and said it wasn't a fall and Garrett had shoved him after they'd gotten into a fight. Though in the end, Jerry Truman was the sheriff, and there was no evidence of Garrett doing anything wrong." Hank put his glass in the sink since I didn't have a dishwasher.

"Really? Jerry Truman was the sheriff?" It came out in a whisper as my thoughts whirled to what Jerry would say if I asked him tonight at the Milkery.

"See." Hank bent down and looked me in the eyes. "That's the look you get when you want to snoop. I know that look. I know you, and I don't want you to touch this with a ten-foot pole, even though I know that will only fuel your fire."

"Natalie needs help," I said as a smug look swept over my face.

"Oh, Mae." Hank tsked. "Funny how you suddenly want to help Natalie." He put his hand out for me to stand up.

"I only want to make sure Natalie keeps away from my man," I joked and stood. "Are you going to get dressed?"

"Yep. Me and Chester." He kissed me and patted his thigh to get Chester to get up. "Let's go eat," he told Chester, "and leave the ladies alone to get dressed."

"True gentleman," I said and opened the campervan door to let them out.

After they left, I checked the corn pudding to make sure it was baking as it needed to and decided to write down all the things I'd learned about Mitchell Redford over the past twenty-four hours in the notebook the Laundry Club Ladies and I used to keep track of such things.

"Fifi, we have some interesting facts that have come our way." I always talked to Fifi as if she were human, and I swear she understood everything I was telling her.

She popped up out of her dog bed and jumped into the café table chair Hank was sitting in. She looked at me intently with her big brown eyes. The pink diamond-studded collar would soon be replaced by a cute emerald-studded collar with a pumpkin pattern on it, and she would be dressed in her little orange puffer jacket for small poodles such as her.

"We have Theodore Redford, who died many years ago along a trail by falling off a cliff." Abby usually took notes in the notebook, but she wasn't here, so I looked back to make sure I was doing it the way she'd been doing it so if—or more importantly when—the ladies and I were together, we could just pick up off where I'd left off and not make Abby redo the clues I was writing down.

I put two circles in the middle of the piece of paper. One had Theodore's name written in it, and the other had Mitchell's name in it. Underneath each one I made a few bullet points before I made several lines coming from the circles to write a name on who might have motives to have killed either of them, even though Theodore's death had been ruled an accident, according to Hank.

There wasn't much to fill in since I'd not had many details, just the few side things I'd overheard, which from Christine, Mitchell had always thought Garrett Callis had something to do with his cousin's death.

"Take in the fact Garrett and Mitchell had the very public fight at the Red Barn Restaurant, it doesn't look good for Garrett that Mitchell turned up dead at the scene when Garrett was supposedly on his way to get his car after he'd gotten out of jail," I told Fifi.

Her little head turned to the side, and her ears perked up as she listened intently.

"The fact that he's missing makes it seem like he's hiding, but none of that makes him a killer." I tapped the ink pen on Garrett's name I'd written in one of the lines leading away from Theodore, since it was initially Theodore he was accused of pushing. "But did Mitchell know something more about the accident?"

That was when I started to write down the questions the Laundry Club Ladies and I would try to figure out.

I continued to write and ask the questions out loud. "Did he hit on something that made Garrett realize this case could be opened as a cold case murder if Mitchell did know something, and that is why he killed him?"

My head jerked up, and I looked at Fifi.

She popped up too.

"Who was Mitchell meeting at the Red Barn this morning? Or was he waiting there for Garrett to pick up his car, and another fight happened?" There were so many questions that I just needed answers to, but more importantly, Natalie needed answers to in order for her love life to continue with Garrett and get her out of my thick, curly hair.

Speaking of hair, I put the ink pen down and pushed my fingertips into the mess on top of my head.

"I need to grab a shower." I stood up and grabbed the bag of kibble from the pantry so I could feed Fifi before we went to the Milkery.

Even though she'd be darting around and out of my sight for most of the time, there would be some people there who would try to give her food, which wouldn't be good for her little digestive system. Fifi was better than any vacuum on the market. She could sniff out a crumb and eat it. No matter if it was on the kitchen floor or the dirt outside, she'd eat it.

My theory was to make her full now so when she did get the opportunity to eat something, she might not. But she was a dog, and I'd never seen a dog give up food. I had good reason to believe my theory would be completely debunked in the first few minutes. At least I tried.

She jumped off the chair and started to eat while I headed back to my small bedroom.

These walls were old wood pallets that I'd turned into that popular shiplap.

I'd used every bit of space possible in the campervan when I'd modeled it by watching DIY videos. In fact, I'd taken down any walls in the campervan to make more of an open feel with the kitchen and family room in one big room.

It was big enough for the cute café table with two chairs from the Tough Nickel Thrift Shop, as well as a small leather couch. It was perfect for two. The captain's chairs made even more seating, so it was good for having the Laundry Club Ladies over.

The floors were redone with a prefabricated gray wood, which made it so easy to clean up anything I'd dragged in by way of my shoes from the campground or even Fifi's dirty paws.

The kitchen cabinets and all the storage cabinets were white. I'd transformed the little camper into a country farmhouse.

The bathroom was where I'd spent the most money by upgrading to a good toilet. Even though the campground had a septic system, I still wanted a nice bathroom with tile in the shower.

My bedroom was so comfy and romantic. Again, I'd gone to the Tough Nickel Thrift Shop to get the perfect used dresser with the distressed look I was going for. I'd also bought a new mattress, because a girl had to have a good night's sleep, plus nailed-together wooden pallets for a headboard that I'd painted pink.

If Hank and I were going to live here, I was thinking the pink head-board would be the first thing to go.

A happy holiday sigh escaped me when my toes wiggled around on the fuzzy rug in my bedroom. It was home, and I still loved it as much as the day I finished it.

I pulled out the dresser drawers with my warm sweaters and decided on a green angora sweater and a pair of khaki pants that were more fitting and would be perfect to tuck into my pair of shin-high brown boots.

First things first, tame this unruly head of hair, and a much-needed shower was called for too. It was more of a way of washing away the day's activities so far so I could try to not think about Mitchell Redford and enjoy a delicious meal with thanks in my mind instead of murder. Plus being around people I loved was really what I was looking forward to most.

Fifi was sitting on top of the bed, on top of my sweater, after I'd gotten out of the shower.

"Fifi, get off that." I shooed her off, but then she went and lay on the pants. "Fine, but I'm going to put those on after I dry this hair."

I padded down the small hallway and peeked into the oven's little window to look at the corn pudding. My mouth watered as I took in the light browning on the top. I could already taste what was under that layer, and giving my hair a light drying would be just the amount of time the pudding needed to finish baking.

With my hair in place with the right products, all my clothes on, enough makeup on to satisfy Mary Elizabeth and a lot of lipstick on my lips, I gave myself one last look in the bathroom mirror before I went back down to the kitchen and took the pudding out of the stove.

"Perfect," I told Fifi. "Now, let's get your coat on and go potty."

She darted over to the basket where I put her coat and sat down.

"You are so smart." It was the baby voice I used that made her tail wag with delight. She loved her clothes, and she made all her outfits look adorable. "We have to change your collar, or Granny will notice."

Even Fifi didn't escape Mary Elizabeth's critical clothing eye.

Quickly, I got Fifi all dressed up, leash clipped on her collar, and out the campervan door. We headed to go on a quick sniff walk around the park before we had to leave.

"Don't someone look s'cute." Dottie smiled at Fifi when we made it up near the recreational center, where she and Henry were sitting at one of the picnic tables.

"Thank you." I grinned and pretended like I thought she was talking to me. "Isn't Fifi cute too?"

"Huh." Dottie snorted. "You know who I was talkin' about."

"Yeah. I know." Fifi and I stopped so she could get some loving from Henry and Dottie, as if she'd not received it daily from them. "Are y'all getting hungry?"

"Hungrier than a tick on a teddy bear." Dottie patted around her freshly dyed red head. "You've not mentioned nothin' about my hair."

"It looks great. But I'm thinking you did it and not Helen Pyle?" I was talking about Helen, the owner of Cute-icles, the only beauty salon in Normal and where everyone went.

"Helen was booked. I barely got me an appointment for a Christmas dye." Dottie wrapped one of her tight curls around her finger. "It's a shade brighter."

"It looks great." I tugged on Fifi's leash so we could finish our walk. "Do either of you need a ride?" I extended the offer though I knew they were probably going to ride together, even though Dottie wouldn't have anyone think they did.

"We'll see you there," was all she said as I followed Fifi down the other side of the lake toward our campervan.

The guests of the campground weren't out. It was very quiet, and the sounds of the creatures running around in the woods made the breaking branches noises and the rustling of leaves. Sometimes the squirrels were so loud, I was sure it was some sort of bear or buck making all the ruckus, but it was generally a squirrel.

Fifi was on a leash because she would've darted into the woods or even jumped into the lake with her coat and fancy Thanksgiving collar on.

Hank's fifth-wheel door popped open as we started to walk by, and Chester darted out. He never jumped in the lake or took off like Fifi. Chester was a hunting dog before Hank had gotten him, and when Hank was on a case where Chester's original owner had died, Hank took Chester. Chester was really good at listening to commands, so the little he had to do to hunt or find, he was all about it.

But he loved Fifi and greeted her by sniffing her new coat. She stood there and let him all proud-like before she finally had enough and nipped at his nose.

"You look beautiful." Hank appeared at the door with a blue-striped sweater on, a pair of nice darker jeans, and some brown loafers.

"You look handsome." I smiled and wondered if we were going to be this complimentary when we were five or even ten years married. "Are you ready to go?"

"Does Dottie or Henry need a ride?" he asked and stepped down the steps, turning back to lock up. He clicked the key fob for his truck to unlock.

"Nope." I shook my head, walking Fifi and Chester over to Hank's truck. I opened the door and picked them up to put them inside. "I'll go get my purse."

"I'll pull up." Hank got in on his side.

My campervan was just a few camping lots down, and he'd already pulled in front of my house before I even walked down there. My keys were hanging on the hook, and my purse was still in the captain's chair, but I knew I wanted to get the notebook to show the Laundry Club Ladies since they were all going to be there.

I stuffed it in my purse along with my phone, grabbed my keys and the corn pudding, and locked the door behind me.

Hank was standing next to the passenger door, because not only was he a gentleman and always opened my door, but he was also guarding Fifi, who would've jumped out in a minute.

Fifi took her spot on my lap after I'd gotten in. I fastened my seat belt and got situated with the corn pudding for the few minutes' drive. Chester sat in the set of seats behind us, looking out the window.

"Are you sure they don't need a ride?" Hank asked when we passed Dottie and Henry still sitting at the picnic table.

"They said no," I assured him before his phone rang.

"Hey, Jerry." The phone hooked to his OnStar service.

"Hey, man. I've got an issue." Jerry's voice cracked or the cell service skipped out for a minute as Hank left the campground on the way to the Milkery. "You know that old Redford case?"

"Yeah." Hank kept his hands glued to the wheel but looked over at me.

"The cousin of that kid was murdered this morning." Jerry talked, and I wondered why Hank hadn't stopped him to let him know he'd already heard. "I'm afraid after all these years there's been some evidence that was overlooked when I had the case that points to the possibility Theodore Redford was murdered."

"What are you saying, Jerry?" Hank cut to the point.

"I'm saying I think the cousin, Mitchell, might've been killed because I overlooked evidence years ago. That would mean this could come back and bite me." Jerry was pretty much saying if the real events of what happened came to light, he could go to prison for withholding evidence. "I'm going to need your help."

And with that, Hank was put in a very difficult position. Either he would help Natalie Willowby or Jerry Truman. A decision only he could make.

CHAPTER SIX

There was a carport added to the back of the Milkery bed-and-breakfast house, where you entered the kitchen. There were tables and chairs set up out there along with one of those fake free-standing fireplaces where Mary Elizabeth added the perfect southern-style fall touches to the mantel.

Fifi and Chester ran off ahead of us after I'd gotten them out of the truck and sat them on the grass. They were good about staying in the yard and not going to bother the cows. Though Fifi did try her hardest to get into the chicken coop every time we came to visit. There was no way she could get in.

"When did she do that?" Hank asked when he came around to get the corn pudding casserole dish to carry for me.

"I have no idea. It wasn't here yesterday, but it's a great idea to have for extra seating." My mind circled back to who she'd invited or was expecting.

Hank went on inside the kitchen while I waited for Fifi and Chester to get finished sniffing all the smells and take a tinkle. Mary Elizabeth's excited voice trailed through the screen door.

Hearing her made me smile. She loved having all this company, and it filled her little southern heart to entertain. Her way, of course.

"She's outside with the dogs," I heard Hank say before the screen door creaked open.

"Just set it on the stove," Mary Elizabeth called to Hank about the corn pudding, and I turned around to greet her as she came outside. "Isn't this a great idea?"

"It is so cute." I greeted her with a hug. "Happy Thanksgiving."

"Happy Thanksgiving to you. What do you think about the mantel?"

She and I walked over to look at the vibrant leaves she'd gathered from the surrounding woods that'd fallen off the trees. They were so lovely with their green bases and threads of yellows, reds, and oranges entwined. She'd even gotten a few buckeyes and chestnuts the squirrels hadn't gotten to fill in little gaps here and there along with a few gourds and tiny pumpkins.

"It'll give people someplace to come and sit, talk and enjoy the beautiful outdoors while they can warm by the fire." She searched the leaves for a small remote control. She pressed a button, and the gas logs lit up. "Instant heat."

"I love it," I said and watched Fifi and Chester rush up to get a gander at what we were looking at. "I wonder if I could get one of these for the tiki hut next to the lake?"

"I don't see why not." Mary Elizbeth tucked her hands inside the front pockets on her apron. "Did you see the table runners?"

We walked over to one of the two banquet tables she'd already decorated for today's feast.

"I got them at that big home store." She ran her hand down one of the runners with the embroidered pumpkins on it. "I can also use them for the inside tables." She wiggled her brows. "Repurpose them."

"I love this one too." I moved to the next table, where she'd used muted-green leaf garland down the middle and little white pumpkins intermittently nestled between the leaves. "This is very romantic. Were you up all night doing this?"

"No. I got up this morning while all the guests were talking about the dead body you found, so I used my nervous energy to get everything ready." She stood behind me with both hands on my shoulders.

"That way you can enjoy your Thanksgiving, seeing this is my last one."

"Last one?" I jerked around and looked at her.

Her straight hair was perfectly in place. The ends grazed the pearls around her neck. They complemented her downplayed look today. She wore a pair of dark jeans and a burnt-orange sweater. Her apron would come off as soon as the guests arrived, and I loved her flat shoes that matched her sweater.

"I'm going to pass the holiday torch to you after you get married." She rearranged a few of the white pumpkins and fiddled with the cloth napkins.

"What about Abby? She would love to host." Hosting holidays didn't sound like too much fun for me. I loved holidays. Cooking, I didn't love.

"It's passed down to the daughter. Besides, Abby and Bobby Ray need to focus on getting me a grandbaby." Mary Elizabeth's thinking shouldn't've shocked me, but it did. "Look how cute this is."

She picked up a medium-sized pumpkin I thought was just a decoration and opened the lid.

"I made it an ice chest. And the thick lining of the pumpkin keeps the ice cold." Her shoulders shimmied with delight before she put it back in place.

"I didn't find a body." I wanted to make sure she knew it. As much as she wanted to move past our conversations by pointing out the various decorations that were adorable, I had to set the record straight on Mitchell Redford.

"I heard it was the jogging folks." She turned to go back into the kitchen, and I followed her. "Aren't you one of them?"

"Christine and I had decided to jog on our own this morning, and when we passed the Red Barn, Al Hemmer and Colonel Holz were already there." I clicked my tongue for Fifi and Chester to come inside.

"Look at that little coat." Mary Elizabeth had grabbed a few of her homemade dog treats from a mason jar that sat on the counter just inside of the door. "Here you go, babies."

They took the treats and ran off to go devour them.

"Speaking of babies." Mary Elizabeth's eyes moved down to my engagement ring. "Have you two thought about this wedding?" She was smart enough to direct her question to Hank and not me.

"You wouldn't believe it, Mary Elizabeth." Hank walked over and picked at the snack-type food Mary Elizabeth had in bowls for people to munch on during her cocktail hour. "She actually said she would like a fall wedding."

"I didn't give a—" I started to talk, but the squeal coming from the depths of Mary Elizabeth's insides made Dawn Gentry come running into the kitchen.

"What's wrong?" Dawn's eyes darted around the kitchen, a toilet-scrubbing brush in her latex-gloved hand.

"Nothing, but if there was something wrong, were you going to scrub them to death?" Hank teased and got up to greet her.

"I don't have a fancy gun like you do." She eyeballed the waist of Hank's pants, knowing he was probably packing a gun under there, which he was. He had continued to keep his gun on him with his conceal-and-carry permit since he'd stepped down from being the sheriff.

"They have the best news." Mary Elizabeth's shaky hands went back and forth from her hair to her mouth as she tried not to let the recent wedding news escape. Then she started to bounce on the toes of her shoes before she exploded like a pressure cooker. "They are getting married next fall!"

Dawn's jaw dropped with a growing smile. She reached out to hug me.

"This is wonderful news, you two," she said and then moved from me to Hank. "Congratulations."

"It will allow me to get some showers planned for our friends in Perrysburg." Hearing Mary Elizabeth even mention Perrysburg made my nerves go unhinged. "All the parties here. And oh my stars." She pulled her lips together. Her nostrils flared before the excitement exploded. "You can get married here."

"Here?" Hank and I both said in unison.

"Yes. Here." Mary Elizabeth spread her hands out in front of her. "Just picture a gorgeous fall day. I bet Bobby Ray will be able to carve some sort of altar that you can take back to the campground to display. Jessica will make the most gorgeous fall floral arrangements and swag to go along the top of the altar."

Jessica Niles was the owner of Sweet Smell Flower Shop.

"Oh, and Fifi. Ethel will fancy her up and paint Fifi's nails." She rushed over and put her hands in my curly hair. "We won't tell Helen, but we will bring in a stylist to tame this."

"This?" My brows shot up as I tried to take the insult with dignity, though Mary Elizabeth never would've seen that as an insult.

"I think you're a little ahead of yourself," Hank finally interjected. "I just got her to say a season. Not a month or a date, but she did say who she wanted to ask as a bridesmaid."

"Who?" Dawn quickly asked, and I could tell by the look on her face she was hoping it was going to be her.

"Hank, dear." The *dear* word came out with a little more oomph so he'd get the hint to stop talking. "It's Thanksgiving, and I'm so grateful we are all here. We don't need to make this day about us. We can do that tomorrow."

For me, tomorrow would never come for this subject, but I knew it was enough to get Mary Elizabeth to agree to.

I had no idea that even mentioning tomorrow would send her into euphoria for the entire day. Not even the second batch of homemade rolls that were a little on the burnt side got her in a bad mood.

Within a few hours, the tables were filled with friends and people I'd considered my family, with full bellies.

Jerry and Emmalyn Truman, Betts and Lester Hager, Abby and Bobby Ray Bonds, Dottie, Queenie, Henry, Hank, Ellis, Hank's parents, along with Agnes had found their way outside, where Hank and I were enjoying a slice of Mary Elizabeth's pie.

Though the turkey should've taken center stage at our gathering, it was the pie table that really got all the attention and taste buds.

"Can I offer anyone some coffee?" Mary Elizabeth walked outside with a tray of mugs and a carafe of coffee. Far from the Styrofoam cups I'd offered at the campground.

A few of us spoke up, and she hurried over to distribute the cup of joe that paired well with the salted caramel apple pie I'd chosen over Mary Elizabeth's famous pecan pie.

"Y'all holler if you need something else." She left us all sitting at the tables underneath the carport as she hurried inside to take care of the rest of the community members who'd also joined us.

"Lester." Hank pulled up his leg and rested his ankle on his other knee. "How have you been feeling?"

"I'm doing all right." Lester looked pale and thin. I did glance at him a few times during the meal to see if he was eating, and he appeared to be. Betts had told me previously his appetite had decreased. "Betts has been kind to make sure I'm doing all the things to make my process go as well as possible."

Without saying it, he was meaning his journey to death. It was quite remarkable and almost comforting to hear him speak this way of the inevitable. Though there were a lot of people who were shocked and unhappy about his pardon, it was done, and there was nothing anyone could do about it, plus the fact he was terminally ill didn't make sense for his victim's family to pursue any sort of reversal on the governor's decision to let Lester out of jail early.

But Grady Cox Jr. was another story. He was the one who'd killed Paul, my ex-husband, though I had no intentions of appealing the decision of the governor for the sheer fact that Grady Cox Jr. had a mental breakdown, which led to his insanity plea to having killed Paul.

His mama, Ava Cox, and I over the years since Paul's death had come to form a good friendship, and I was glad to hear she'd taken Grady Jr. to get some much-needed treatment at a facility out of the state for a few months.

I had high hopes he'd get the necessary treatment for him to have some sort of full life.

"She comes over to the apartment every morning with the day's food." Lester looked at Betts, his eyes almost skeletal. "I'm grateful to her and to you for allowing me to come to Thanksgiving."

The sincerity in his voice was felt, and the group he was sitting among had been his good friends and loyal congregation at the Normal Baptist Church. Though we all seemed to take his insight on us welcoming him today, we all never agreed to accept what he'd done.

But he would know the mind of a killer and why someone would've killed Mitchell, which I would definitely use as a benefit. Then there was Jerry. His presence didn't go unnoticed. Especially after his phone call to Hank on our way here a few hours ago. I'd kept my eye on Jerry, and there was a lot of fidgeting, uneasiness, and looking around.

"How do you like the new preacher?" I asked, knowing Lester had been volunteering down at the Normal Baptist Church and helping out with Brother Alex Elliott.

Alex Elliott came from the biggest bourbon distillery in Kentucky, so to say the congregation of his hire approved by the elders of the church was somewhat shocking would be an understatement.

There were snide comments made about how the fake grape juice given out for communion was now going to be replaced by bourbon and how he would get his hands into the political ring of counties that were still dry in the state, which were many, but so far, he'd proven he was a simple man of God.

Mary Elizabeth had mentioned him a million times when she'd tried to get me and Hank to get to church on a Sunday. Sundays were the busiest in the campground with the leaving of the week's guests and the arrival of the new guests. But I'd had some dealings with Alex, and he did seem to fit the bill the church needed to step into new leadership.

"He's a good man. He's young." A faint smile crossed Lester's face as though he had a memory. "Remember those days?" he asked Betts.

"I sure do." She laughed and tucked a strand of her wavy brown hair behind her ear before she folded her hands in her lap. "Lester and I thought we were going to save the world. One Christian at a time. And looks like it broke us."

Silence fell over the group, but leave it to Dottie to liven it back up.

"What did I tell y'all years ago about that Garrett Callis?" Dottie brought up the subject of the murder of Mitchell Redford. "I told y'all he was no good. He came from no good. He was brought up from no good. But he thinks he's something, and after all these years, it's come back to him." Her eyes narrowed behind the cigarette smoke. "He thinks he's somethin' too."

"Do you really think he killed Mitchell?" Abby asked.

"Do I think it? Huh." Dottie took the cigarette from her mouth and held it in between her fingers, pointing directly at Abby. "I told Jerry Truman that boy did it years ago, but did you do anything about it?"

The folding chair Emmalyn was sitting in groaned when she shifted uncomfortably.

"I did." Jerry cleared his throat and vigorously rubbed his hands together.

"I wasn't asking for a response, but here we are years later after that boy's death, and now we have another one on our hands after Garrett and Mitchell had that public fight." Dottie shifted her focus to Hank. "I'm telling you, last night Garrett was standing in that parking lot, talkin' to that floozy Natalie, who if you ask me still wants you." She waved her cigaretted hand in the air. "But that ain't what we're discussing here. I'm telling you that you need to find the Garrett boy and shake him a few good times to see if anything comes out of that head of his. I swear," she spat, "I'd like to buy that boy for what he's worth and sell him for what he thinks he's worth."

Dottie was so passionate about Garrett Callis there was a feeling there was more to the story than what we were discussing at this moment, which was making everyone a little uncomfortable.

"From what I understand, they don't know where Garrett is, and bringing up a past death isn't going to solve this one." Hank directed his comments to Dottie.

She flung her leg over top the other and started to swing it like she was in a kickball tournament.

"Just like Jerry always said, the facts are the facts." Dottie knew she was fueling the fire, and I wasn't sure why, but I trusted Dottie. She might not have a filter, but when she spoke as passionately as she'd done just now, I knew there was something deeper, and getting it out of her would have to wait until later tonight when we were back at the campground.

"Now they have better equipment and technology than the words of people." Jerry put it in a nice way how Garrett Callis was exonerated. "I never figured it to be Garrett who might've had anything to do with Theodore's death but the other kid that was there."

"Harrison Pierce," Queenie spoke up. She'd been so quiet, I'd almost forgotten she was there. "His mama was in my Jazzercise class the day it happened. I remember his sister coming in and getting her. It actually stopped the class."

"It was the first child of our community to have died on a trail in as far back as I can remember," Emmalyn recalled. "The kids who grow up here are very well trained in the dangers of trails. And drinking on them. I think that's why it was so hard to wrap our heads around what happened. An awful time in our life that I will never want to revisit again."

"Who all was there that night?" I asked. "I guess if something did happen to Theodore and he'd not slipped over the cliff, one of them would know something. Seen something."

"They all had the same story. The exact same story." Jerry nodded. "It was odd then, and it seemed like they'd rehearsed the story. I could never break them, but there was one time when Harrison paused."

"Paused?" I knew this was a good tactic to use when trying to get information out of someone, if you wanted them to keep talking because you knew they had information you wanted but they didn't want to tell you.

The slight pause was so uncomfortable for them, it was like the words would crawl out of them, and that was when they'd tell you things or clues they hadn't realized were clues. It was the pause during these questions that led to the truth.

"Yeah. He paused. Then he started backtracking and fumbling around. He lawyered up and hid behind the safety of his attorney. We never got clear evidence the accident was any more than that." Jerry was a good sheriff and one very well-liked by the community, but not everyone here knew he'd called Hank about this very thing.

He sounded much different now than he had when he was on the phone, which told me he was hiding something. Maybe something from back then jarred his memory, or he recalled something from back then that didn't seem so important and now it would be considered a major clue.

"During that time Jerry had his hands full. The rangers were on strike, and the sheriff's department had to deal with all the incidents with tourists. All the kids in town were drinking." Emmalyn used her fork to pick at her piece of chess pie. "Remember they had to shut down the only liquor store in town because Rex Pierce was letting Harrison take whatever liquor they wanted."

"Oh yeah." Jerry snickered, rolling his eyes and fiddling with his coffee cup. "I went to see Rex after the accident and let him know the kids told me how Harrison was the one who provided the liquor." Jerry frowned as the disappointment settled on him. "He said he had no idea Harrison and his friends were doing such a thing."

"Come to find out, weeks later, another kid in the community with a different set of friends had to be flown to a hospital in Lexington due to alcohol poisoning." Emmalyn filled in the gaps Jerry was leaving out, and I was mentally taking notes.

I glanced at Dottie and Queenie to see if they were listening. Betts was totally listening because she kept kicking me underneath the table.

"When that kid finally came through, he told Jerry he was able to waltz right on into Rex's liquor store and get whatever they wanted," Emmalyn said as she placed her hand on Jerry's arm. "Jerry had to go confront Rex, and since no one had died and everyone had recovered from the alcohol poisoning incident, Jerry pretty much told him to shut down the business, or he was going to get sued by the family of the boy."

"Is that true?" I asked Jerry.

"Yeah. It wasn't as simple as Emmalyn is making it out to be. I did put some deputies out front of the liquor store to watch a few weeks while the kid was in recovery because it'd done some brain damage, causing him to require some inpatient physical therapy. I hated it, but it bought me some time to get a handle on what was going on around here." He shot a glance at Dottie. "Don't you remember he was at the board meeting and how mad he was."

"As sure as I'm sitting here, I remember." Dottie tapped the butt of her lit cigarette on the ceramic ashtray Mary Elizabeth had sitting on the table, clearing the ash. "It 'bout nearly keeled him thinkin' these youngins' were getting all looped up over Rex Pierce wantin' a dollar or two."

"What ever happened to them?" I asked.

"Which ones?" Jerry needed me to clarify.

"Both." I wanted to know the outcome.

"Last I heard, Rex was living off Knights Spring down by the rock quarry," Jerry said then finished, "He started working there when he closed the liquor store. The boy, heck. I have no idea what happened to him."

Queenie cleared her throat. The Laundry Club Ladies and I looked at each other, knowing this kid was one of the first people we'd be looking into if we were looking into it. Jerry's cell phone rang a text.

"What was that boy's name?" Jerry's brows knitted as he looked at Emmalyn before he looked down at his phone.

"Carson Rivera." Agnes broke her silence. "His family lives in that fancy architect-designed home on Red Hill Pines."

"I've been dying to go in that house." I'd heard of the architectural marvel since I'd lived here but never ventured out there.

Though it was only five miles from the Happy Trails Campground, it actually took over thirty minutes to drive due to the nature of the roads through the mountainous forest to get there.

"It's something to see." Agnes gave me the look that told me I needed to talk to her but in private.

Agnes, Hank's granny, was the sheriff's department dispatcher among other tasks since the department was so small everyone had to pitch in where they could. Agnes was good at letting off little hints about different crimes I'd gotten involved in. Not only did we get along really well, we also worked alongside each other even better when it came to our duty to keep Normal safe. Even if we played armchair sleuths.

The fireplace gas logs flickered, dancing some light on her face, making her saggy jawlines appear a little deeper than usual. Agnes had short gray hair and was in great shape for being in her eighties.

"It appears Mitchell Redford wasn't murdered. He was killed due to a severe allergic reaction to wasps." Jerry was reading his text, and he didn't mention who it could be from. He was so well connected to the community due to the fact he'd been the sheriff for years. It could've been anyone from the mayor to the coroner.

Laugher spilled out the screen door of the kitchen, and soon thereafter, Hank's parents and Ellis had emerged with an armful of tinfoiled plates.

"Someone is going to be eating good tomorrow." Hank stood up. So did I.

"Tomorrow?" Hank's dad patted his belly. "Heck, all these might be gone by midnight, son."

They gave each other a hug, then his dad gave me a hug.

"Your mama spilled the beans about next fall," Hank's father whispered in my ear. "I'll try to hold off Hank's mama as long as I can," he warned.

I pulled back and smiled at him. He was always so kind even though his wife had yet to accept me as the daughter-in-law. But Hank didn't care. He was already harboring ill feelings against her for picking Ellis as her obvious favorite, as she took Ellis all over the country to try to make Ellis a model and star while she left Hank here in Normal to be raised by Agnes.

In truth, it was a blessing. Hank had gotten his sense of gentlemanly manners and his personality from Agnes. To me that was the most important part of him. His kind heart. Don't get me wrong, he was a tough cookie to penetrate to get to know, but he was loyal to the end if he was in your corner.

Everyone from outside must've taken the cue it was time to pack up and get home. They all funneled inside. All but Queenie, Betts, Abby, and Dottie.

"Dear." His mama grinned, though it wasn't sincere. Her cheeks balled, and her eyes were blank. "Thank you for a lovely evening, Mary Elizabeth. Mother." She darted a look at Agnes.

"Night!" Dottie called, speaking up for Agnes.

"Ready?" Hank's mama sucked in a deep breath, looking between Ellis and Hank's dad.

"We will see you soon." Hank hugged his mom and his sister and then walked them out to their car. Agnes followed them as well.

When Hank and his family had turned the corner of the old farmhouse, Queenie swiftly turned around.

"Are we on this or not?" She didn't even need to explain what she meant. She was talking about Mitchell Redford's murder.

I nodded.

"I can't help but wonder why Natalie Willowby would go to Hank and ask him for help with solving the murder before Mitchell's initial autopsy was released." I looked between them. "Something seems off. I don't know what it is, but it's sitting right here." I pointed to my gut.

"Are you going to ask him?" Abby asked.

"Ask him?" I smiled. "Nah. He's got enough on his plate. I can ask Agnes to see if she can get us a copy of Colonel Holz's initial report. I'm not convinced Mitchell's death was an accident."

My words seemed to latch on to the chilly fall breeze and carry through the screen door into the kitchen.

We all turned to see who was coming out.

Dawn Gentry.

"Did I hear you guys talking about Mitchell Redford's murder?" she asked in a shaky voice.

"Jerry Truman got a text that said Mitchell wasn't murdered." Dottie always loved to deliver such news. "I reckon our…" Dottie was going to say something before Dawn spoke up.

"I know for a fact he was getting death threats." Dawn stunned us with her information, leaving the Laundry Club Ladies standing there with our mouths hanging open.

CHAPTER SEVEN

D awn's news had changed everything the Laundry Club Ladies had thought about the text Jerry had received. We told Dawn to come to the Laundromat in the morning after the annual Turkey Trot so we could discuss what she knew and see if it really was information Al Hemmer needed to keep the case open.

It wasn't that we didn't believe her, but there was nothing we could do about it tonight. It was Thanksgiving, late, and I had to be up in the morning to join Christine on the Turkey Trot I'd signed up for. Not that she would be keeping pace with me, but I honored my commitment.

"You're awfully quiet." Hank noticed my silence on the way back to the campground after we'd helped Mary Elizabeth and Dawn clean up from the Milkery.

Mary Elizabeth always made sure she cleaned up after the last guest left, and she didn't care if it took her well into the night to get it all done. With the four of us chipping in, we had it done in a few hours, including taking down the tables and chairs underneath the carport and putting them back in storage at the Milkery's office that was away from the bed-and-breakfast.

"Dawn Gentry mentioned something about being friends with

Mitchell Redford." I wasn't sure what Dawn had heard when we'd gotten further into conversation before Hank and Agnes had come back after they'd walked Hank's family to their car. "From the way she reacted to the news of Mitchell's cause of death, she was pretty upset and certain it was murder."

"Why would she say that? I've never seen Colonel Holz wrong," Hank said.

"He could be right but possibly overlooking something." I stroked Fifi, who was sacked out in my lap. Chester had found a place between me and Hank in the front seat of the truck. "Could someone use wasps as a weapon?"

"My gosh, Mae." Hank gasped and turned the truck onto the gravel drive of the campground.

The old wooden sign with Happy Trails Campground etched in it was something I'd not changed when I took over. It fit the landscape, and it was iconic to me, so I kept it but had Henry shore up the posts by adding more concrete and stability so a good wind wouldn't knock it out.

The gravel spitting up underneath the truck tires made Fifi and Chester pop to their feet. They recognized the sound as home.

"Why on earth would someone do such a thing? That would be premeditated murder." He slowed his speed way below fifteen miles per hour then parked in the spot in front of his fifth wheel.

It was late and pitch dark, the way we loved to keep the campground at night so the guests could see all the gorgeous landscape and the sky. It was one of the reasons a lot of campers came to the Daniel Boone National Forest, to get out of the city. If there were lights, it would ruin any sort of spectacular views from orbit, and tonight all the stars were out.

Even the moon hung over the lake, showing off the calm water that invited me and Hank to take a seat in the Adirondack chairs on the edge of the lake between our campers.

Fifi was on her leash, sniffing around us, while Chester stuck close to her, checking out what Fifi had just given some attention before they both moved on.

"She said he was getting death threats delivered to his house." I looked at Hank.

He blinked several times.

"Why would someone want to kill him?" Hank asked a question we all wanted to know, if it was truly murder. "Not that we are going to do anything about it, but I say everyone needs to let Colonel finish up his report before anyone goes blaming anyone for murder."

I nodded and smiled, being the good fiancée and pretending he had a great idea.

In the pit of my stomach, I knew I couldn't just let Dawn's information not be taken seriously here on Thanksgiving. After all, Thanksgiving was an action word, and there was some action that I would be looking into after tomorrow's Turkey Trot.

"I better get to bed. I'm meeting Christine at the starting line." I leaned over and kissed Hank before I slipped the end of Fifi's leash off the arm of the chair.

"I'll be at the finish line, cheering you on." Hank looked up at me. "Are you sure you don't want me to take you in the morning?"

"No." I'd told him several times over the past couple of days I'd drive myself. "Let Fifi out for me before you come. Please."

"Of course." He sighed and patted his belly. "I think I'm going to sit here and enjoy the fresh air while my food digests a little more. I'm too stuffed to lie down."

"I'm going to tear into those leftovers after the race tomorrow." I used my fingertips to scruff up his hair before I started to walk back to my campervan. "I can't wait to eat a bigger piece of pie," I called, leaving him laughing.

Fifi took another minute or two to sniff around the camper before she decided her nose had had enough and waited at the step of the camper as I opened the door. I glanced back at Hank and for a moment had a vision of us walking home together. As one. As a married couple and not going off our separate ways down the campground.

My phone buzzed with a text in my purse, and I snickered, thinking it was him sending me a goodnight text.

It wasn't a text. It was a phone call from Waldo.

Quickly I picked up Fifi and put her in the camper before I walked inside and shut the door behind me, answering the phone at the same time.

"Hey, Waldo. This must be important for you to have called so late." I'd left the boundary door open a few months ago when I was trying to give the poor guy a chance and teach him how to live in the community where no one trusted the journalist.

"Did you hear the news about Mitchell's death being wasps?" He immediately started in on the recent news.

"Wow, how are you getting this news so fast?" I asked.

"You asked me to be in the community, and Colonel gave me some information tonight." That was interesting.

"How did you get information from Colonel?" I had to know.

"Being with the *Normal Gazette* isn't the best-paying job in the world, so I took a job down at the funeral home as a greeter. You know, the person who stands at the door and opens it as people come in?" He didn't need to explain. I knew what a greeter did for a job during funerals. "We've gotten to know each other a little since he works closely with the funeral home. Both of us like hunting and fishing. He's in the hunting club, so he invited me to go bowhunting a few weeks ago, and it opened the door for me."

Bonding over hunting. Ugh. That was something I was never ever going to do.

"I am not a good hunter. Really, I don't try because the thought of killing something really isn't my nature, but for a good tip or story, I can shoot a gun and deliberately miss."

"You said you bonded over hunting and fishing." I wasn't making the connection after he said he was not killing anything.

"I can talk about it enough to make it seem as though I know about it. I can shoot a bow and a gun, so there's that. Listen, I'm saying there's more to this case than wasps. I don't know what it is, but he said the man was stung over fifty times. That's a lot of wasps." Waldo was only making the statement I'd asked Hank about wasps as a weapon. "Trust me when I say I notice everything when I go to a scene. It doesn't mean it's a crime scene but even just a break-in. I didn't see any wasp's nest when I was at the Red Barn Restaurant."

"What are you saying exactly?" I didn't have time to listen to his ramblings. I had to get to bed.

"I'm saying someone had to have trapped Mitchell Redford into a wasp's nest. They knew he was allergic to wasps, and if he wasn't armed with his nebulizer after being stung, which why would he bring it to a bar when wasps really shouldn't be living in the colder climate, or they have them in a place where it's nice and warm." Waldo was making my loose theory even more solid.

"We need to find out if anyone is raising wasps or has some indoor facility where they took Mitchell, let him get exposed to the wasps." My voice trailed off as the theory started to come together in my head like a puzzle.

"Trapped him." Waldo finished my words, leaving me with a more chilling image than I'd had before. "Like a greenhouse or something."

Greenhouse.

Who would have one?

Garrett Callis's family.

CHAPTER EIGHT

My body physically groaned when I bent down to touch my running shoes. I raised my arms over my head and leaned side to side in hopes to warm up not only my muscles but my body.

"Can you believe this weather?" Christine jogged in place with so much energy. Her shoes left an imprint in the light dusting of snow that'd gathered on the sidewalk in front of Trails Coffee.

"I heard it was going to snow." I shook my head. "I've never run a Turkey Trot. Nor have I run in snow."

"I hope the mayor had the Kentucky Department of Transportation out there salting the roads or at least getting brine on them." She took a little jog over to the jogging group. Her entry number flapped against her back.

She wore an orange tutu over top her jogging pants with little turkey faces all over them. Christine took the look and the run seriously. I couldn't help but wonder if the headband with the two springs attached with the bobbling turkey legs was actually going to stay on the entire run.

I looked completely boring with my black joggers and Happy Trails T-shirt on, though I wished I'd worn the sweatshirt, even though I would've gotten rid of it in the early parts of the run, since I'd be panting and sweating to death.

Not from the run but from the thoughts of me trying to finish before next Thanksgiving.

"Go, Mae!" I heard the familiar voices of the Laundry Club Ladies as they stood near the coffee shop behind the starting line, holding signs that were of my face. "We know you can do it!"

"Oh jeez." I gulped and watched as the group of real runners lined up, since they must've known something I didn't. I fell in line in hopes to just blend in.

I had no idea what happened, but all of a sudden, the herd of people moved forward, me along with them, and before long, we were running past the shops along the downtown area.

Apparently the race had started, and I was dead last, though I did have to look in at the Tough Nickel Thrift Shop display because Buck had put out some of the Christmas things he'd been holding off on putting out until after Thanksgiving.

There were a few trees in the window I knew would look great for the campground. I had to make sure I got those before anyone else. Too bad my cell phone wasn't on me or I'd have called Dottie or Henry to go buy them.

To say this was the dumbest idea ever was an understatement. It wasn't enjoyable at all. I could hear Dottie in my head already about how she'd told me this was not a good thing to do.

My stomach grumbled because it was hungry, my feet ached with each landing, and my legs killed me with each stride. My lungs felt like shards of glass were poking them.

"My goodness." Gert Hobson greeted me at the finish line. "For someone who only did the minitrot, you sure look like you're in pain."

The Laundry Club Ladies were darting through the crowd to get to me.

"Mini or not, I have come to recognize running just might not be the thing to keep me in shape for my wedding." I felt the tingly red bumps come up on my legs. "I need a coffee and a doughnut."

"Coming up!" Gert, the owner of Trails Coffee, hurried off as the girls came up.

"You did it!" They all greeted me with huge grins and pats. Even Dottie. "You ran three miles!"

Three miles didn't sound like a lot, but it was a lot to me.

I hugged each one of them and loved how they all dressed up for the occasion.

Queenie had her short hair tucked up under a headband that looked like she'd made it out of construction paper with different colored feathers stapled on the back.

Abby had on a pair of sunglasses in the shape of red leaves and a costume jewelry necklace strung with plastic turkeys.

Betts had on one of the Turkey Trot marathon tees they sold at the registration table, and Dottie had on a black shirt with a bedazzled turkey on the front.

"Dottie." I grabbed her arm. "Did you see the Christmas trees?" I was going to ask her about the Tough Nickel Thrift Store.

The other ladies went over to the courtyard of Trails Coffee and grabbed us an outdoor café table right underneath one of the heating lamps.

"May-bell-ine." She waved a hand and shook her head. "I saw it this morning and thought the same thing. Henry already packed them up in the truck."

"We make a great team." I hugged her, and it just felt right. The right time to ask. "Will you be one of my bridesmaids?"

"Whut?" She drew back, her eyes all big and round. "I think we need an oxygen mask over here!" she hollered and pointed to me. "May-bell-ine West Grant has lost her ever-lovin' mind!"

"Stop it," I said. "I'm serious. I want you to be right there like you've been for the entire time I've dated Hank."

It was true. The day Hank zoomed his big FBI car up the gravel drive of the campground, where he accused me of harboring Paul after Paul had escaped prison, then with him deciding to be a ranger, where I put my nose in many of his cases, before he became a sheriff, when he wanted to arrest me for interfering. She was there for all of it. Even the happy moments.

"If it weren't for you, I'd not be engaged." I reminded her how Hank wasn't really proposing the day he gave me the gorgeous emerald ring. He was simply giving me a gift, but Dottie hooted and hollered how he was proposing in front of everyone at the campground.

Hank was all for it when I was trying to stop Dottie that day. I quickly realized I, too, was happy, and it was perfect the way it'd happened even if it wasn't how Hank initially wanted it to happen.

"Besides, you truly are one of my best friends. Why would you not think I'd ask you?" I held her hands in front of us.

There were tears in her eyes.

"I'm an old lady. I can keep the guest book or something. Unless your bridesmaids' dresses need a little glitz." Her chin cocked to the side, and she gave me a wink. "I can bedazzle anything."

"I'm serious." My face stilled, and I looked into her eyes. "But no smoking down the aisle, and you can't carry your cigarette pouch."

"I reckon I better start puffing now to make up for it." She dropped my hands and took out her pleather cigarette case.

"So that's a..." I hesitated. "Yes?" I asked cautiously.

"I reckon it is," she muttered with her eyes narrowed as she lit up the lighter, puffing the cigarette to life.

I threw my arms around her.

"Whoa! Don't be going and getting burned. That's the last thing I need to be accused of is burning the bride." Dottie pulled away. She wasn't the mushy type, and hugs drove her nuts, but deep down, Dottie was an old softie.

"Come on." I moved through the crowd. "I need a doughnut."

The Laundry Club Ladies and I sat at the café table, having our copious amounts of coffee, and I did eat two doughnuts, which might've used the calories I burned jogging, but I would imagine I ate more doughnut calories than I'd burned.

Hank had joined us, and one by one, all the real marathon runners started to trickle in. The winner was from out of town and was walking around with the turkey crown wrapped up in what looked like a big piece of tinfoil.

There'd not been any more snow, but the gray clouds and the meteorologist told of snow showers to come.

Waldo Willy had cornered Mayor Courtney McKenzie in the grassy median between the two one-way streets of downtown.

She didn't look like she was enjoying the interview, which made me wonder if he was asking about Mitchell Redford.

"Any news from Natalie?" I asked Hank.

The folding chairs underneath the Laundry Club Ladies groaned as they leaned into the table, resting on their elbows, shoulders up to their ears.

"No. I haven't tried to call her." He leaned back for Gert to set a hot cup of coffee in front of him. "Thank you," he said to her and picked it up, blowing on it.

"Do you think she's found him, and that's why you've not heard from her?" Abby asked.

"I left it with her to let me know if she did hear from him or if she wanted to proceed. I'm not sure I'd be able to find anything out, but I do know I can track his last whereabouts, which I'm sure Al Hemmer is already doing." Hank didn't give specifics into how he'd handle Natalie's request.

The Laundry Club Ladies did things a whole lot differently. We snooped around until we got a clue with some meat on it, then we gnawed at that meat clear to the bone until it was validated or just a rumor.

As we sat there, more and more runners from the trot crossed the finish line, but not Christine. I did see Will and a couple of the others from the group.

"Excuse me." I gripped the handle of my coffee; my hand was still shaky from the mini run. Run was used loosely. I'd never tell my friends, but most of the time, I'd considered my pace a fast walk.

The group of runners were comparing their times and talking runner talk. None of which I understood, but it was fine because after today's epiphany about how being a runner wasn't my thing, I put any and all terms—even the schedule Christine and I had—way in the back of my mind.

"You're drinking coffee?" Will looked at me like I had three heads. He lifted his water bottle with his fancy electrolytes in it up in the air. "You really need to hydrate properly."

"I'm fine." If he only knew my innards required a healthy dose of coffee every morning, he'd probably faint right there. "Did you see Christine? She's not come in yet."

"No. We pulled out of the pack around the quarter mile." He looked at the group, and his face stilled. "You were back there with Christine, right?" He pointed to one of the other girls.

"Yeah. She got a cramp and told me to go on," she said without any concern.

"Do you think I need to go look for her?" I wondered. Christine was really good at keeping up with the group on the other days, unless they'd picked up their speed for this race.

"I'd give her some time." The lady continued, "She said her knees were locking up, which can take some time or make you go much slower than normal."

They didn't seem concerned and went on with comparing their times, throwing out some suggestions on how they could do better with new techniques to try in the morning.

I slipped away and headed back to the group when an orange tutu caught my eye.

Relief fell over me when I saw those darn drumsticks flailing in the air, still on top of Christine's head.

I ran to the finish line, forgetting about the coffee in my hand. It sloshed inside the mug and burned my hand before I finally tossed the liquid into a garbage can as I passed it.

"Go, Christine!" My words caused her to find me in the screaming crowd. The freckles on her face widened along with her smile before it gave way to a grimace.

Instead of waiting at the finish line like the rest of the spectators, I ran back across it to meet her and encourage her to finish if she wanted to.

"Are you okay?" I asked her and grabbed her arm to throw around my neck. Her groan was enough for any words. "Lean on me and we can do what I did. Fast walk if you can."

"I can." She panted. "I swear I've never had such bad cramps in my life."

"We will address that in a minute." I didn't want her to use her energy and what little gumption she had left in her to waste on talking.

And in a few short seconds, we were across the finish line.

"Here you go." Hank appeared out of nowhere with Will.

They each had something for her: Hank had the typical banana for a runner after, and Will gave her a bottle of the electrolyte water.

Hank took her from me and helped her ease down on the curb in front of Trails Coffee. Not the best place to sit because people were walking all around us, and there were some vendor tents for running equipment set up for this event.

I joined her on the curb while Will and Hank stood in front of us like bodyguards. Out of being nice, Hank drummed up a conversation with Will about running before he outed me about my decision that running wasn't for me.

"Don't worry," Christine said. The empty banana peel dangled between her tented knees. "I think I'm going to take a much-needed break. Stick to hiking the rest of the season."

"You can go on any new trail suggestions I get." I smiled and patted her. "I'd love to have company, and it's really great exercise."

"Sounds great." Christine's head popped up as the crowd in the street parted. "Excuse me." She stood up, steadying herself by holding on to my shoulder as she got up.

Hank saw someone he knew, and he walked over, giving the guy a handshake and a smile before they plunged into a deep conversation.

As a board member of the National Park Committee, there were always emails coming in of suggested trails hikers would find in the woods. Most of those were deer trails, which helped out so we didn't

TRAPPING, TURKEYS, & THANKSGIVING

have to create new trails, but we'd enhance them if they did fit the criteria.

I was the one who was given the task to check those trails out using the coordinates given in the email by the hiker. On some occasions, I'd ask the hiker to accompany me if it was an area I wasn't familiar with, but in this case, I'd love to have Christine come with me.

She would be really helpful. There were different criteria for trails to be approved and placed on the maps of the Daniel Boone National Forest. Things like the difficulty of the hike, if there were any specific landmarks or features like a lake, stream, waterfall, or just anything in nature, such as amazing views.

The forest was so large, we'd not begun to touch it and see the beauty it truly had to offer.

"Who is that?" I asked when I stood up and got a view of the man Christine was talking to.

I gave a slight head nod.

"That's Harrison Pierce." Will's mention of the name sent me right back to yesterday's Thanksgiving supper when Jerry Truman had mentioned him and his father Rex.

"Did his dad have a liquor store?" I asked in hopes to get some information from Will since he grew up here like Christine and knew everyone.

"Yeah, but he wasn't on the up-and-up." Will shrugged. "I've not seen Harrison in years. He still looks the exact same."

"Were you friends with him?" I asked.

"No, but my cousin was. And Christine." Will smiled at the fond memory. "I was the little cousin who tried to tag along but was seen as a pest." His laugh reached his eyes. They sparkled as he talked. "Theo used to invite me to some things but not a lot. I think our moms made him."

There was a moment of silence as we both looked at Christine and Harrison. Both of them looked to be catching up.

"Christine was always considered to be just one of the guys. I know that sounds terrible, but she was always athletic and wanted to do all the sports. She was really good at football, and I don't mean the flag or two-hand touch." His brows shot up. "She'd leap and tackle anyone."

"She is a really good person," I said and watched her twisting around in a flirty way.

Christine didn't have a boyfriend, and maybe this little Thanksgiving reunion would spark something. Or they could've been talking about Mitchell.

"She's been a great friend to a lot of people." Will smiled.

"You said Harrison hung out with the group." I tried to slip in any conversation I could when trying to find clues to a murder, and though technically I wasn't snooping into Mitchell's death, it didn't hurt just in case. "He must've known Garrett."

Will nodded, not giving any sort of emotional look or body language to clue me in on if they were friends. So I poked more.

"Did they get along?" I questioned in case Harrison knew where Garrett's whereabouts were.

Think about it. If one of my best friends had come to town while I was being questioned for a murder, why not hide out wherever they were staying? It seemed like something someone on the lam would do.

"They were the closest among the group. Why?" Will asked. "You think one of them killed Mitchell, don't you?"

"I'm not saying that." I shrugged and was never so glad to see Ethel Biddle in my life. "Ethel!" I called to get her attention. "I'm sorry. I need to go talk to her about Fifi's grooming appointment."

"We will miss you at the running group." He smiled. "You can join anytime you want."

"Thanks, but I think I'll hang up these running shoes." I snorted and excused myself just as one of the other runners came up to Will to drag him over to one of the vendors to show him some sort of running shoe.

It looked like every other running shoe to me, though I bet it was something special and new.

I kept an eye on Harrison in hopes to get a little face time with him and Christine after I made small talk with Ethel.

"Can you check to see if Fifi has an appointment this week?" I knew

I'd scheduled something to make sure Fifi had her nails painted and hair cut for my upcoming Christmas card photo shoot.

"We can go look now if you want." She gestured across the median to where the Smelly Dog Groomer shop was located.

When I looked, I noticed Harrison Pierce was walking away. As in, away from the crowd and away from downtown.

"Call me," I told her and hurried off in his direction but not quick enough before I saw him get into a car.

My running day wasn't over yet. I sprinted across the median and down the sidewalk past the Laundry Club Laundromat to jump in my car in pursuit of Harrison Pierce.

CHAPTER NINE

H arrison knew the roads well. I could tell he'd driven them many times because he was able to hug the curve of the road, going at a good clip of speed without braking around even the biggest hairpin curve that ran alongside one of the deepest cliffs of the forest.

I gripped the wheel and let up on the gas to make sure I did make it around the curve. Once out of it, I pushed the pedal of my little Ford to at least be in sight of him.

When I didn't see him, my heart started to beat with anxiety. Did he see me? Did he turn off? All sorts of ridiculous ideas popped into my head. Then I wondered what Christine had told him and if it possibly scared him off from hanging around downtown.

He wasn't a runner, so why was he there?

I'd already heard that killers liked to join in on activities in the community after the murder due to the fact their ego side gets a sick kick of enjoyment hearing people talking about the murder.

Was this the case?

Puffs of chalk from a gravel drive caught my attention, and when I stopped shy of it, I noticed the brick mailbox. A cemented name was encased on the side.

Callis.

Harrison had brought me right to Garrett's family home. Was Garrett hiding out here?

"Surely Al came here first," I muttered and decided to take my chance to follow Harrison's car to see what I could find out.

Harrison's car was parked, and he wasn't in it. I parked next to him and got out.

I looked around to check out my surroundings. I grabbed my phone from the passenger seat and left the keys in the ignition as I got out of the car.

"Can I help you?" I heard a voice come from the side of the house. It was Harrison.

"Hi." My lips quivered a smile and then drew in a thin line, bouncing back and forth between the two since I wasn't sure what I was walking up on. "I'm here to talk to Garrett."

"I'm here to find him." Harrison stuck his hands in the pockets of his jeans. "Who are you?"

"I'm a friend of Christine Watson's." When I mentioned her name, his body relaxed, and his face softened.

"You're the crime-solver-type person but not really." He didn't seem to have the words. "You fixed up the old campground."

"Yeah." I nodded. "How did you know?" I asked.

"I saw Christine at the race, and she told me all about Garrett and the whole Mitchell thing." His eyes lowered. "She pointed you out. Did you follow me here?"

"Maybe." I gnawed on my lip. "It's part of that whole crime-solver-type-person thing." I used his own words to explain why I was there.

"I see what you did there." He smiled. "I tried calling Garrett, and he didn't answer. I talked to him at the Red Barn the other night. He said his parents had gone to visit family out of town, and he was staying here. Then he told me about him and Natalie Willowby, which shocked the heck out of me."

There were so many things I needed to break down in his observation, so I started with the burning question first.

"Why were you shocked about him and Natalie?" I asked.

"Let's say he was never her type. No one's type, as a matter of fact. Well, one guy…" His voice got quieter when he realized I was the one guy's girl. He looked down at my hand. "Sorry. Christine also told me you were engaged to Hank Sharp."

"And that's the guy?" I asked.

"You know. Natalie and Ellis were always together. In my opinion, Natalie was always a little jealous of Ellis and how the Sharps catered to Ellis." He shrugged. "But I don't care about all that. I just want to make sure Garrett is okay."

"I didn't see you at the Red Barn that night." I only had a few sips of the cocktail before the fight broke out, and I wasn't a big drinker anyways, so I remembered who was there and who wasn't.

My memory was not cloudy. I knew I'd not seen him.

"I left before Christine got there. I'm sorry. I don't remember if I saw you or not," he apologized.

"I showed up after." I wanted to talk to someone who was there earlier than me, and unfortunately, that was probably Natalie. "Did you know Garrett was arrested for hitting Al Hemmer?"

"Yes. Natalie called me asking if I knew where he was because he might be a suspect in Mitchell's death. Which I'd heard he died from wasps. He and Theo were so allergic to wasps." He did have some news for me to chew on.

"Really?" I wanted to hear more. You never knew when someone recalled something years after the incident.

"I don't remember all of it. After all, we were kids. But I remember every time we went somewhere, Theo's mom made sure he had his EpiPen thingy with him." His lips ticked up. "I do remember in elementary school when we were dangling from the monkey bars, a wasp came out of one of those little holes in the metal and stung him."

He sucked in a deep breath. His face showed emotion as though he were still hanging from the outdoor play equipment.

"He swelled up so big and so fast. I'd never seen anything like it. The teacher didn't even know what was going on, but the school nurse had an EpiPen and injected him." He did the motion of jabbing the skin.

"That's when they found out he was allergic. That weekend, all of our parents from my group of friends gathered here, out back in the greenhouse."

"Here?" I wondered why they would come to the Callises' house.

"Yeah. Mrs. Callis has that big greenhouse in the back. She lets all the bugs, wasps, bees, and snakes in there to keep the plants healthy. Theo's mom said she wanted to show all us boys what Theo was allergic to so we could inject him with the EpiPen," he said.

"That's really smart." I was impressed.

"Think about it. A bunch of boys and Christine played out in the forest all day. You come up on wasps all over the place here." He told of a lifestyle most children didn't get to experience in nature due to the fact the Daniel Boone National Forest was their backyard.

"Anyways," he continued. "I came here to see if Garrett was hiding out here. Natalie said she checked, but I thought I would check. I don't think he killed Mitchell Redford."

"Mitchell Redford was sure Garrett killed Theo." It was time to change the subject, and this was the perfect lead in to ask about the pause during his statement Jerry Truman had talked about the other night.

"No. Heck no." He shook his head. His forehead and nose wrinkled. "No way." He vehemently denied the accusation.

"I was talking to Jerry Truman the other night." I watched as his body stiffened and his chest rose.

"You know what." He stalked past me, going back to the side of the house where he'd come from. "I'm not going to do this with you. You've wasted your time following me out here."

"I'm trying to help. That's all." I didn't want to leave just yet. Besides, I wanted to see if Garrett was here.

I tried to keep up with Harrison as he picked up his pace once we were past the house and heading toward the large greenhouse I'd heard about. We were talking huge. Like two barns big.

Nothing I'd ever seen in public.

"Your friend Jerry Truman didn't help at all. He put my family in the poor house. He shut my dad's business down without even trying to let my dad recover." He spit out the words over his shoulder at me but kept walking.

"Your dad was selling liquor to minors." Abruptly, I stopped when he did so I didn't smack into him.

Slowly, he turned around and gave me the most evil look.

"Listen, I don't think you should be here any longer." He fisted his hands and turned back around to keep going toward the greenhouse. "I'll tell Garrett to call you when I find him."

"You'll what?" I asked just as a dark cloud came over us, and sprinkles of snow started to fall from the sky.

"This is why I left here." He stopped, threw his hands in the air, and looked up at the snow.

"What did you say about Garrett?" I asked.

"I told you to go," he said through gritted teeth and started to walk again. "I said"—his voice was a little louder—"I'll tell Garrett to call…"

There was a hesitation in his steps, and his eyes were forward.

I looked past him to see what caught his attention enough that he couldn't finish his sentence.

"Garrett!" He darted off in a sprint with his eyes on the greenhouse door that was propped open by Garrett Callis's body.

Lifeless body.

Garrett wasn't going to call anyone.

Anymore.

CHAPTER TEN

"Call an ambulance!" Harrison Pierce frantically barked orders at me.

"Don't touch him." I tried to get him to stop moving Garrett's body. I'd always heard when you happened upon an injured person or a possibly dead one, you didn't move them unless they would benefit from CPR.

Only problem here, Garrett was dead. His skin was gray, his eyes were open, and his lips were blue.

"Come on, man." Harrison talked to Garrett as he eased him down on the ground to start chest compressions. "I told you to call the ambulance."

There was no reasoning with him, so I did what he said.

"Agnes." I was so happy to hear her answer the dispatch.

"I was figuring on hearing from you by now. I've got the file for you," Agnes whispered in the phone, obviously not wanting someone standing near her to hear.

"Agnes, I need you to listen to me." By her silence, I'd grabbed her attention. "I'm at Garrett Callis's parents' home, and I think, um, know he's dead."

"What?" she hollered.

"We found him propped up against the greenhouse door. He's dead. Can you send Al?" I asked.

She muttered a few things before I heard her call over the police scanner to find Al and get him here. Only she called all available units as well.

Before I knew it, Tucker Pyle was standing in front of me and Harrison Pierce as we all stood over Garrett Callis's cold, dead body.

"Who are you?" Harrison's anxiety seethed from him when he noticed Tucker.

"Tucker." I didn't have too much time to explain due to the fact Harrison was still determined to bring Garrett back to life. "He's a ranger."

Tucker bent down next to Harrison and put a hand on his back.

"I was the closest, but the ambulance will be here soon." Tucker was able to assess Harrison's reaction and respond to the fact he'd not accepted the realization of Garrett's fate. "Why don't you let me take over?"

Harrison hesitated.

"You go over and stand with Mae. If there is any way I can bring him back, I will, but you doing all of these chest compressions will only break more ribs." Tucker used gentle words and facts that clicked with Harrison.

Tucker moved to the other side of Garrett's body and put his arms out to take Garrett from Harrison.

When the arm on Harrison's side fell to the ground, I noticed there was something green in Garrett's grip.

"What on earth is going on around here?" Harrison ran his large hand down the front of his face as though he were trying to wipe away the scene playing out in front of him.

The whirl of sirens was chillier than the landing snowflakes that were now falling in large clumps.

"I have no idea, but I do know everyone will be getting to the truth, and we might have to ask you some very serious questions that will be hard but will help the authorities bring the killer to justice."

"Killer? You think Garrett was murdered?" Harrison shot me a look as if he'd not even thought of it. "There's no blood."

There was a screech as several tires slid to a halt behind us. We heard the noises that would eventually lead the deputies, the EMTs, and Colonel Holz to the scene.

Oh. And Waldo Willy.

The EMTs hesitated when they got to Garrett's side. The type of pause where they knew there was literally nothing they could do. Tucker gave them a slight nod before he circled his eyes over to Harrison.

The EMTs understood what Tucker was telling them and quickly went about the normal activities they'd do if they were able to bring someone back from the dead, but from the looks of the greenery still in Garrett's grip, rigor mortis had begun to set in, because his fingers didn't open at all.

"Maybe he does have some fatal wounds we can't see." I pointed out the fact Garrett had on a heavy coat along with boots and jeans.

There were two EMTs, one on each side of the body. They looked up from their stethoscopes and shook their heads before they glanced up at Tucker.

"Oh my." Harrison got choked up on his words and hid his face in his hands and started to cry. His shoulders jumped up and down as he tried to hold it in as much as he could.

"I'm so sorry." I ran my hand up and down his back for some sort of comfort, only to have him jerk away.

Colonel Holz had already bent down to get an initial look at the body and to see if he could see anything that stood out.

While he did that, I walked away from Harrison to give him some time alone and found myself right next to Waldo Willy.

"Let me guess." I looked at him blankly and tugged the edges of my coat up around my neck to ward off the frigid temperatures. "Police scanner?"

"Yep. If they don't want people here"—he glanced over his shoulder —"they shouldn't broadcast it."

I followed his gaze, and when I did, the deputies had put up a body police line to hold back some of the citizens who'd come to see what the call was about.

"May-bell-ine! May-bell!" Dottie waved her hand in the air, the trail of smoke from her cigarette following in line. "Come here!"

Betts, Abby, and Queenie were with her.

She took a step forward, and when the deputy put his hand out, she smacked it away.

"Don't you touch me. I know your mama, and she didn't raise you like this." Dottie started to shame the young deputy only trying to do his job. "I ain't goin' nowhere, so you head on over yonder." She swatted at him again and curled her nose before she looked at me. "May-bell-innne!"

"Hold on," I muttered and put a finger in the air. I wanted to see what Colonel Holz was going to say with his initial findings.

Al Hemmer had showed up without me even realizing he'd gotten there, and when he bent down, Colonel whispered something in his ear, and both of them looked at the greenhouse.

Everyone was busy doing their own thing. Even Waldo was scribbling down notes, so I took the moment to slip off to the side of the greenhouse and search for an entrance.

My phone buzzed, and I quickly hit it to make the sound shut off.

"Whut is goin' on?" It was Dottie. "I see you walkin' away. Who's dead?"

"It's Garrett Callis, and I'm not sure if he was murdered or what because there's no visible wounds," I whispered. "The only thing I could tell from Colonel talking to Al was they both looked over at the greenhouse, which makes me think they are going to check it. I'm just trying to get there first. I can't do that if you keep yelling for me or calling me."

"Fine, but once you know somethin', you come over here because Abby has some news she found while working." Dottie hung up on me, letting that little bit of information hang.

It was like she was dangling a piece of pumpkin pie in my face, and I couldn't eat it until I got back with her.

The greenhouses stood next to each other, and I found myself in between them, peeping in the foggy glass walls to see if I could spot anything. There was a cracked door halfway down the one where Garrett's body was propped up against the door.

Careful not to touch anything and regretting I'd not gotten my winter gloves out from the storage unit at the campground, I used the toe of my shoe to open the door enough to slide inside. The door didn't close behind me, and it was the taller grass that'd kept it open.

It made me wonder if this was how someone had gotten out. I didn't know much about greenhouses, but I'd think the doors should be kept shut.

Something to check out for sure.

There were rows and rows of little green plants. They reached various heights and different shades. When I went down the aisle to see if I could get anything, any clue whatsoever, I realized the wooden sticks with the handwritten words on them were all vegetable-type foods. Some names I recognized, and others appeared to have a different name but, from what I gathered, was some sort of hybrid-type vegetable Garrett's mom was testing.

"Ugh," I groaned when I stepped into some potting soil.

It wasn't just the potting soil all over the floor, but it was the entire tray of whatever was missing from the table with it.

I bent down to look at the wooden label and shook my head when I read it.

"Yuck. Spinach." Just the thought of it gave me the creeps.

I've been told Mary Elizabeth makes the best wilted spinach with garlic and bacon grease, but I was never one to try it.

"What do you think you're doing?" Al Hemmer had turned the corner of the aisle I was standing in. "Goodness gracious, Mae," he scolded me.

"I'm looking for clues."

"How do you know we are too?" he asked and glanced back where Colonel had appeared behind him. "What is that?"

"It's just spinach." I shrugged and went down to pick up the small sign.

"Don't touch it!" Colonel practically shoved Al out of the way to hurry down to meet me. "Spinach," he gasped and slowly shook his head.

"What?" Al had joined us.

"The small hole I found on Garrett and the small amount of foam in his mouth along with the leafy greens." His eyes shifted to the side. He started to gnaw on the inside of his cheek as though he was carefully noodling what he was about to say. "I think he was poisoned. He knew he'd been poisoned, and the way to counteract it would be to eat spinach. Garrett knew it. Only he wasn't able to eat enough to save him."

"The hole was from a needle?" I questioned, and both of them looked at me.

"How did you get in here?" Al tried to maintain his curtness with me.

"The open door." I pointed across the aisles to show them. "Do you think Mitchell Redford was here and stung by the wasps to knock him out or paralyze him in a way? Then someone poisoned him through an injection too."

"They disguised the injection using the wasps." Al started to get the hang of the what-if game.

"I think he had someone inject him first because some of the longer labs are coming back, and his organs had some hypoxia due to carbon monoxide binding of hemoglobin, preventing transport of oxygen, and we did find some rat poison." Colonel looked around and continued like I understood his jargon, "I wonder if he was injected with the poison, died, and then put into a swarm of wasps."

"Who are we talking about?" Colonel and I looked at Al with disbelieving looks on our faces.

"Mitchell," Colonel and I informed Al at the same time.

"Okay, got it, but what about Garrett?" he asked.

"I'm not sure, but I wonder if the tests are going to show this theory." Colonel was all about the science.

"If we can trace Garrett's steps after he left jail, maybe he happened upon the person who killed Mitchell." I was letting my theory fly.

"If he was murdered." Al put a dent in my thoughts. "We don't know that yet, so don't be going and telling your nosey friends out there."

I ignored him.

"Maybe he went back to get his car, and that's when he saw someone with Mitchell?" Something buzzed past me, and I swatted at it without thinking. "Bee?"

"No." Colonel jerked around. "Wasp."

All of us suddenly stopped and watched this wasp buzzing around us. As it got closer, we all bent back to avoid it stinging us, then we swerved to the side before it took off.

All of us had the same idea to run after it to see if there were more.

Al threw an arm around me to move past me.

"I'm the sheriff. I'll go first." He loved throwing his little title up in my face, but the truth was he didn't want me to get the first look so he could say he found the evidence.

He plucked his walkie-talkie off his utility belt and punched the button to life.

"I want you to tape off these greenhouses and the entire property from the mailbox to the edge of the woods." He clicked off to take a breath. He had another thought once we followed the wasp to the far back left corner of the greenhouse, where the wasp burrowed itself back into a five-foot-long wasp's nest. "Get the crowd off the property now."

"We need suits on so we don't get swarmed!" Colonel yelled after a few wasps found their way out of the hive then more followed.

The three of us nearly bowled each other down in order to hightail it out of there before we became the next sting victims.

CHAPTER ELEVEN

"Not that it makes a difference now." Abby sat on the couch of the Laundry Club Laundromat with some papers in her hand. She set them on the table in exchange for our sleuthing notebook we used to keep track of any and all clues from our snooping experiences.

"These are the articles from when Theodore Redford's accident happened," I said after I'd picked them up to look through them.

The bell over the laundromat dinged, and we all turned to find Lester Hager.

"I thought we could talk to Lester about that time." Betts cleared her throat. "I know it might be uncomfortable for him to be here, but I think he has some valuable information to share about Theo's accident."

"Which to me was never an accident, but I wasn't able to say anything due to the fact I was a preacher and kept what was confidential between me and the parishioner." Lester took his skill of being a great secret keeper to a whole different level now that he wasn't a man of the cloth.

"Why don't you just park it right here." Dottie snorted and elbowed me to move, patting the space I'd just occupied.

"Thank you." Lester didn't take up too much space because he'd always been a thin man. Maybe a little thinner now.

"Anyways, I was saying how Theodore's autopsy shows wasps had been the source of his death and falling off a cliff." Abby pointed to the papers on my hand. "They are stapled together."

I pulled the autopsy report from the stack of printed pages and flipped to the diagram of the body, where the coroner marked on Theo's diagram showing a hole the size of a syringe.

"Look at this." I put the papers on the coffee table.

Betts quickly moved all the mugs out of the way so we could all crouch around the table and not knock the coffee on the papers.

"This is what the coroner said was an injection."

I pushed the paper aside and picked up the autopsy finding's report and showed them what I was trying to say.

"Theo was also allergic to wasps."

"Family genes. You can't outrun 'em." Dottie eased back.

"No. That's not it." I got her attention again and pointed at the paper. "It says here Theo had died of an overdose. But I think he was killed by someone injecting poison."

"That was a time when a lot of drugs were going around." Lester nodded. "And when they came out with that report, I thought so too, but when I had the boys for student Bible study, I didn't ever see signs of any sort of illegal drug use, and it didn't add up."

"Right," I said and continued to look at Theo's autopsy report. "Mitchell's body was stung all over with wasps, but I bet when Colonel finalizes his autopsy, there's a suspicious injection site."

"You think someone did to him what they did to his cousin all these years later?" Abby wondered and looked away. She turned back to us after she paused. "But why now?"

"I don't know." I wasn't finished telling them my theory, but I knew we'd get to it.

"The reunion at the Red Barn maybe brought some stuff up, and now that Garrett is dead, the killer was at the Red Barn and overheard them talking about Theo?" Queenie threw out a good suggestion.

"I think it might be some of that. I also think it goes beyond." I cleared my throat to get to my point. "I've tried to think over and over who was at the Red Barn, and while I don't know all the guys Theo and Mitchell hung out with, I do know Christine Watson was one of the group members. Harrison Pierce was my most likely suspect because he was in the group. His dad supplied the alcohol."

As I continued to talk, Abby was scribbling down all the information we were talking about, which told me she was taking all the notes we were going to need to figure out who we needed to check out. It was beginning to appear as if we were once again going to throw our sleuthing caps on to not only move along the investigation but scratch our little curious itch.

"I honestly thought Harrison Pierce was the killer, but both of us showed up at Garrett's family home at the same time, and he found Garrett dead." I sat up, and this was when I really shocked them. "I think Garrett went back to the Red Barn to get his car. He either saw Mitchell get killed or Mitchell was dead. Instead of getting his car, he ran through the forest, using the trail, which leads right to the back of his families' property."

I glanced around, and everyone's wide-open eyes told me they were along for the ride.

"Garrett hid out in his mom's greenhouse to make sure the killer didn't follow him," I said. "He didn't have his phone because Natalie had it. So he couldn't call for help. Or at least she had it when Al hauled him to jail."

"The killer followed him back there and injected him?" Betts asked.

"I think so, but the greenhouse where Garrett was found was the vegetable greenhouse, and he had a fistful of spinach in his grip plus some in his mouth." The only one who caught on to what I was saying was Abby.

"Oh my gosh, Mae. He knew he was injected with poison, so he ate the spinach to counteract the effects or at least buy some time." Abby talked and wrote at the same time.

"Are you tellin' me that spinach cures stuff?" Dottie asked. "I was never good in science class."

"Yes. It won't completely take out all the poison, but it'll buy you time to get some help." Abby was always so knowledgeable and brought so many facts to the group. "Book nerd." She giggled.

"So who are our suspects?" Betts cut to the chase.

"I would definitely put Harrison on there." Lester grabbed our attention. "Out of all the boys in the group, he was the one who always gave Mitchell a hard time about Christine."

"Watson?" I jerked to look at him. "Why?"

"All the boys fell over her, and I'm sure she's too sweet to tell you about it, but there were a lot of fights that broke out in the undercroft while they were there for youth group." The wrinkles around Lester's eyes had met his forehead dips. "But that's not my only suggestion."

"Who else?" I asked and started to go through the list. "We had Mitchel and Garrett, who are dead. You mentioned Harrison, but he was with me when we found Garrett."

"But was he really with you all day?" Queenie got up from the floor, where she'd been looking at the old autopsy report Abby had copied. "What if he did kill Mitchell and never figured on Garrett showing up? Just like you said, he ran behind Garrett down the trails, and from what I can tell, those boys spent a lot of time on the trails and probably knew them very well."

"Queenie." Betts pushed herself up and mimicked the neck-roll movement Queenie was doing to move her body. Then they moved on to arm rolls. "He followed Garrett to the greenhouse, killed him, and ran back down the trail to get his car from the Red Barn."

"He was at the Turkey Trot when I followed him." I couldn't leave that little detail out. "I saw him talking to Christine."

"Was he nervous? Fidgety when he was talking to her?" Betts asked.

"No, but he did drive terribly fast for those roads, but in the snow especially." Mentioning snow caused all of us to look out of the window to see what the weather was doing.

Each year at the mere mention of the white stuff, we all would go into snow mood and head our separate ways to make sure we had our shovels, plenty of salt bags, gloves, knitted hats, along with all the heavy coats plus our boots. Not today.

We were too involved with these murders to even care about the snow that was falling even harder than when we'd gotten to the laundromat to make a sleuthing plan.

"Which makes me think he stopped downtown to be seen." Abby expanded on Betts's theory. "While Garrett was dying of poison. Only, Harrison didn't realize you were going to follow him, so he hurried back to the Callis house, where he wanted to make sure Garrett was dead."

"He never figured the Laundry Club Ladies would be on him." Dottie tapped her temple with her fingers that had the unlit cigarette nestled between them.

"I think all of this is good, but there's one more person you need to talk to." Lester sighed as though he was gearing up to tell us.

"Spit it out, Lester," Dottie spoke in a harsh, raw voice. "I've got to go smoke."

"Jerry Truman." His response made me look at Abby.

She looked at me with a spark of something indefinable in her eye. There was something going on in her head, a memory possibly, from the suggested person of interest that Lester had sparked.

"Jerry Truman did want to talk to Hank about something, and he did mention Rex Pierce and the kid who had alcohol poisoning from the liquor Rex's father had sold him." My foot tapped on the floor as I tried to recall the name.

"The Riveras." Lester spit out the name. "Their son was also in my youth group, and the parents came to see me many months after their son's death."

"I remember them." Betts gasped. "They blamed that entire group of boys for their son's murder because it was Theo who gave him the first bottle of liquor, if I recall. I haven't see Rex in years."

"What?" This was a whole 'nother direction for the killer to be one of the Riveras out for revenge.

"I can't remember everything, but I do clearly remember Maria telling Ryan it was ultimately the boys who got their son drinking along with their friends, but I can't remember the entire story." Betts shook her head. A look of disappointment settled in her eyes. "I'm sorry."

"Don't be sorry. We will put them on our list to go have a little chat." I shrugged, and Abby nodded, writing down all the information. "Where do they live?"

"I think they got divorced quickly after we met with them for counseling." Betts frowned. "And I'm not sure where they live now."

"That'll be easy to find." Queenie put her hands on her hips and rotated left to right in a fluid motion. "Maria is a Jazzercise student."

"When will you see her next?" Abby asked.

"I have a special class this afternoon to help burn off those Thanksgiving calories. All the tryptophan in that turkey really does do a number on ya." Queenie did some standing toe touches.

"What time?" I asked in case any of us could go.

"It's at three." She looked up at the clock that read ten o'clock.

"That'll give me time to get Dottie back to the office and me some time to snoop around before I go back to the office to get Dottie." I had a plan.

"I can't do no Jazz-err-cise." Dottie walked to the door. "I've got a bad hip."

"That hip was fixed, and you can do low impact." Queenie wasn't going to let her off the hook for being lazy. "It'll do you good, Dottie!" Queenie yelled as Dottie walked outside to smoke. "It will do her good."

"I know. That's why I'm going to bring her," I said. "We have one more thing to consider before we decide who we need to see first."

"What?" Abby flipped through the notes she'd already taken.

"Dawn Gentry said she knew for a fact Mitchell was getting death threats. I need to go see her about that," I said and waited for Abby to stop writing. "What do we got?"

This was the time we needed to break down our suspect list and find out who had the most motive.

"We have Maria and Ryan Rivera. Rex Pierce had sold their son the liquor. They have motive, according to Lester, because the group of men in question were their son's gateway to drinking, which took him from them," Abby read from the notebook.

"That will take some searching around for the father's address. But I'll be at Jazzercise in case Maria shows up," I said.

"I can search databases for Ryan's new address. And I'll be more than happy to go with you." Lester was really trying to become part of the group and give helpful information.

"Great," I agreed. "Shoot me a text when you get the address, and we can make plans then."

We all looked at Abby.

"We need to see Dawn Gentry about what she knows and if Mitchell had any sort of idea who was sending the notes." Abby mentioned a good first starting point. "Jerry Truman."

"Oh. I can go do that while I'm here." I gestured out the window where Trails Coffee Shop was located across the streets and the median, since Hank and Jerry's private detective office was located in the back of the coffee shop. "Plus I need to get some more coffee from Gert for the hospitality room." I picked up my mug and took a sip. "Who else?"

"Harrison Pierce obviously." Abby named three people, then she threw a loop. "You can question his dad, Rex."

"Interesting." I never looked at the father as a suspect. "He might have some motive because his business was taken down, though he contributed to it."

"But did he tell the boys not to tell? What kind of life is he leading these days? When a business goes under and it's your livelihood, I can't imagine you forget it." Queenie moved on to waist bends and touched her toes.

"And I need to make a pit stop to see Agnes and Colonel." I wasn't hearing anyone offering to help me with talking to people but Lester.

When a group of people came into the laundromat, Betts went to greet them. They handed her six big bags of dirty laundry. She talked to them like she'd already made arrangements for them to pick it up this afternoon, which meant all my friends were working today. Even Dottie, which gave me the day off.

We alternated days, and today was her day in the office, though it should be super slow.

"Okay." I held my hand out for the list Abby had made. "I'll work my way down these as I can, but I'm going to need the address," I reminded Lester before I glanced down at the list, knowing who I really wanted to talk to first because I knew he had more information than he was willing to share.

Jerry Truman.

CHAPTER TWELVE

It was a special time of the year, and the lingering deaths of Mitchell Redford and now Garrett Callis loomed over Normal, Kentucky, like the gray snow clouds that'd gathered over all of the town.

The murders were cold and chilly like the air surrounding me as I walked across the street through the median so I could go to Trails Coffee.

Dottie had hitched a ride with Lester back to the campground, which gave me some more time to get started on the list we'd made as possible suspects.

"Mae!" Harrison Pierce was sitting on a bale of hay with a to-go cup from Trails Coffee. "I've been waiting for you to come out of the laundromat."

I glanced around to see if anyone else was there to see me talking to him, just in case it wasn't safe. After all, he was a suspect on our list, and so was his dad.

Was he really just pumping me for information? Did he kill the others, and was that why he wanted to know what I knew? I was careful how I reacted to him.

"I really do think they killed my friends." He shook his head as if he were trying to shake off the disbelief. "That's why I need to talk to you."

He put his hands in his pockets, making me tense up in anticipation if he had a gun or worse, syringe, and was going to stab me because he knew I was on to him.

I swung my purse off my shoulder and gave him a good whack in the arm.

"Ouch." He jumped back. "What was that for?" His hand produced a business card.

"Sorry. I thought you might be trying to kill me." I felt really stupid after he held out the card. It was one of Agnes's from the department. "Agnes sent you?"

His brows darted up as far as they would reach on his forehead.

"I can't believe you think I killed them." His jaw dropped. "Unbelievable." He ran his hand through his hair and turned around while shaking his head. His bottom lip curled over his teeth as he appeared to be thinking of a good response. He sucked in a deep breath. "This lady seemed pretty confident you could help me."

"I'm sorry, but you can't help me being a little on edge. I trust Agnes, and I have a lot of serious questions to ask you before I agree to anything." I wasn't about to tell him how the Laundry Club Ladies and I had taken it upon us to snoop around, anyway.

I pointed to the bales of hay up near the amphitheater in the grassy median, away from the others in the park that'd gathered to take in all the fall decorations and enjoy the light falling snow that only added to the gorgeous backdrop.

He nodded, and he put his hand out for me to go ahead of him. Still a little leery, I waved for him to go first.

The wind whipped down the mountain and scuttled across the tops of the big oaks standing in the park, shaking off what few leaves were left. They descended with the light snow in a magical way.

Our feet shuffled among the leaves covering the ground along with a few crunches on the way to our seat.

I kept my eye on Harrison in case he was going to pull a gun or a syringe.

"I trust Agnes, so if she gave you this business card, she must've been telling me you're on the up-and-up with information. Unless you stole it and came up with a grand scheme to kill me." There was no sense in me sugarcoating what I was thinking.

He stopped and turned around.

"You honestly think I killed my friends." He glared at me. "So does the sheriff, and that's why I'm asking for your help. I don't want it if you don't believe me. I need someone who is going to get down and dirty to figure out who set me up."

"I'm going to need to know every single move you made from the time you left the Red Barn last night until this second." I sat down on the bale of hay and gestured for him to sit on the one across from me.

There were some children laughing in the background, who were playing on the stage of the amphitheater while the parents shivered in the cold offstage.

Coke Ogden, Helen Pyle, and a few of the other ladies from the Beautification Committee were already taking down the fall-colored twinkling lights from the pillars of the amphitheater along with the potted mums and garland and the carriage lights dotted around the grassy median.

When I saw Ty Randal, the owner of the Normal Diner and a year-round resident of Happy Trails, join them with a ladder, I knew they were gearing up to get the Christmas decorations up.

Normally my heart would flutter with excitement for all the fun and festivals Christmas brought to town, but right now, I wasn't having any one of those happy thoughts or feelings.

Determination to find out who was the real killer set into my bones, and for some sick reason, it gave me such a high to run after these types of crimes and figure them out.

"I went to the Red Barn, and after that, I went to hang out with Shannon, the waitress from the diner." Harrison was bent over with his forearms resting on his thighs. He turned to his right and glanced over to where the diner was located. "I met her when I was there eating, and she seems like a nice gal. Strange family dynamics, but hey, everyone's got a story."

"Did you go down to her family compound down in Belcher Bog?" I asked, since I'd been there once myself.

"Yeah. They are nice people, but I went there to see what it was all about. She didn't want to go to the Red Barn Restaurant for the old times' sake meetup, so I decided why not do both while in town?" He shrugged.

"Did you two hit it off?" I wondered more than it mattered.

"She's nice and all but not really. Then I went to my room at the Old Train Station Motel. I got up this morning and had breakfast at the diner. Talked to Shannon for a while. I saw an old friend." He sat up. "Christine told me about Mitchell. She also mentioned how Garrett was missing, so that's when I left her and went to Garrett's mom's house."

"And all these people can say you were with them?" It was a matter of me making a few phone calls to see if his alibi shook out. He didn't appear to be showing any sort of the usual signs of lying, like fidgeting, looking away from me, or fiddling with something like fingers, hair, or whatever, and there didn't seem to be any physical flinches either.

"I gave them all to the sheriff too," he said. "That's when the old lady gave me her card and said to talk to you. Then she laughed about you being a tough cookie or something."

"Agnes and I are close." This was also a good time to put going to see her on my to-do list. "I can't guarantee I'll find anything out that you don't already know, but I might have a few leads to where this might go."

He stood up, and I did too.

"I have to ask one thing though." Jerry Truman's comment about when he interrogated Harrison when Mitchell Redford had fallen off the cliff. "Jerry Truman told me you had hesitated when he was questioning you when Theo fell off the cliff."

His body language changed.

"It was interesting how everyone had the same story about what happened. Down to every single detail." I opened my bag and pulled out the file of papers Abby had printed. "Here is the public file with everyone's statements. Everyone included where the sun was that day, making it hard to see."

I shuffled the papers between the witness of their group and pointed out how everyone had described the scene the same way.

"Don't you think it's odd and almost calculated how every single one of y'all had the exact same descriptions of even the little piece of slippery moss along the trail?" I continued to show him everyone's words written right there on the page as I felt his body stiffen next to me.

"I hesitated because I didn't know if I should tell Sheriff Truman, um, Jerry, how Garrett insisted we all tell the same story." Harrison came clean. "Because I'm not sure if Theo really did slip. He and Garrett were arguing."

"Over?" I asked.

"Who was the better hiker. Stupid kid stuff. We were in high school, and even though we saw Christine as one of the guys, you can look at her and tell she's not." He pointed out the obvious. "None of the guys wanted to date her, but they all wanted to impress her when we were together."

"Even you?" I asked.

"No. I never had a big sense of ego." He looked down at his body. "If you were to see a photo of me from back then, I was a scrawny kid. Most of us in that group were kinda outsiders anyways. That didn't help matters that a girl like Christine would hang with us and not some of the jocks."

"Here we are today, me and you and the rest of the gang." I put the files back in my purse. "Theo is dead. Mitchell is dead and now Garrett. Do you know anyone who would have any cause for the truth about Theo to come out?"

"You pointed to my family. My dad earlier, but everything was already taken from us when… when…" His voice trailed off. "Did you know the Riveras sued my family with a civil suit?"

"The kid who got injured after he'd gotten liquor from your dad's store?" I wanted him to know I knew the case.

"Yes. They sued us and left my family with nothing." He shuffled the leaves around his boots. "That's why I left town. I needed to get away. Make a clean break from Theo's accident, then that kid's."

"How would your dad feel if I stopped by to talk to him about Carson Rivera?" I asked.

"My pops died a few years back. Alcoholism." He snorted. "Selling alcohol or drinking alcohol was going to kill him one way or the other."

"I'm sorry to hear that." I was sorry to hear that I was going to have to cross off Rex as a suspect, leaving me questioning if Carson's family was plucking these kids off one at a time. "Do you feel unsafe?"

"Heck no. I just want to find out who killed my friends, why, and go back to my life away from here," he said. "Are you going to help out?"

"I told you I'd look into it." I patted my bag. "As you can see, I've already started to gather some information."

Talking to him, I used words that made it sound like I was a true professional instead of just a snooping campground owner.

"I'll be in touch." I turned and quickly headed across the street, where I stopped briefly to look at the new display window at the Tough Nickel Thrift Shop.

The Christmas trees were in one of the storage units at the campground, and now Buck had one of those electric indoor fireplaces in their place with stockings hanging from the mantel with different winter accessories and tools hikers would love to have for winter hikes.

All things were slowly turning into a winter wonderland now that Thanksgiving was behind us, but I sure wanted the Christmas feeling I was used to tickling my innards.

Yesterday the Thanksgiving Day banners hung from the dowel rods of the carriage lights along the sidewalk. Now it was Christmas wreaths with a flickering candle in the middle of them that made downtown glow for what was to come in the next few weeks.

With the forecast predicting it was going to be a much snowier winter than usual, the idea of a winter wonderland really did come with a much-welcomed soul.

While I took my time walking past the few freestanding cottage-style homes with a small courtyard between them that'd been turned into the cute shops, I thought about what Harrison had told me.

There were so many unanswered thoughts that I knew one of Gert's hot cups of coffee would help clear my mind and get me thinking on the right track.

Trails Coffee Shop was busier than normal for a middle-of-the-day time, but with the weather as cold as it had dropped and the few flurries whipping around, coffee must've sounded good.

"Hey, Mae!" Gert Hobson, the owner of the coffee shop, greeted me when the bell over the door signaled my arrival. "I got your order ready."

"Thanks. I'm going to need a strong cup of coffee too." I looked at the living wall she'd had built with live plants she switched out year-round.

The wall was made of gorgeous and thriving succulents, miniature conifers, ferns, hyacinths, crocuses, and snowdrops. It was so pretty and festive. I knew everything around me was screaming Christmas, but my insides weren't.

"Your coffee is over there for the baskets," Gert called out from behind the counter. She had a to-go cup in her hand filled with a fixing of that strong coffee.

I had an agreement with many of the local businesses in Normal. I only used their products in my campground. I served complimentary coffee from Gert alongside the Cookie Crumble's doughnuts or scones or muffins in the recreational center at the campground. The guests were also offered many different baskets to purchase with various local goodies in them. For instance, if they wanted more coffee, for a small fee, they could purchase a coffee basket that featured Gert's specialty coffees and treats. If they wanted a spa kit, which were very popular with the girls' weekends, they could purchase a basket put together from Cute-icles. It was my way of giving back to Normal after what my ex-and-now-dead husband, Paul, had done to the town. In turn and just because the people in Normal are good, the area businesses put Happy Trails Campground flyers in their shops and even in customers' bags.

It truly was an amazing community, and I was proud to now call it home.

"There you are." Hank snuck up behind me. "I was going to get a cup of coffee to go for you and give you a call to bring it to you."

"Anything in particular you wanted to talk about?" I asked in hopes he was going to say something about the case or Natalie or both.

"I was thinking about how much I love you and our life." He wrapped his arm around me and gave me a nice big hug.

"I did want to tell you something." I wanted to tell him about Harrison and how he'd asked me to help him, which made me take him off my little list of suspects.

"Excuse me!" a man in the coffee shop called out and was pointing at the television Gert had on in the back of the counter. She liked to keep it on with the volume low for the weather report and the hiking trail report offered by the National Park so hikers and campers were well aware of the conditions at all times. "Do you mind turning that up?"

The man was standing at one of the long farm tables with a group of others. The tables were great for larger gatherings, and Gert had made them all so cute.

In the middle of them, Gert repurposed old bourbon barrel lids and made really cool lazy Susans out of them. Each one had little containers of different condiments you'd need for any type of coffee. It was like each table had its own little coffee bar that could just be twirled around to make the perfect cup of coffee.

"It's Al's press conference," Hank said, uncurling his arm from me.

He and I both walked up near the glass display case to see what Al was going to say. Gert had set the cup of coffee for me down and turned up the volume.

All chatter and noise stopped inside of the coffee shop as all ears and eyes were on Al.

"First off I'd like to thank the sheriff's department for quick actions on what had taken place at the Red Barn Restaurant with the murder of Mitchell Redford." There was some chatter in the background on the television, which were reporters asking him to confirm the murder, though we'd already heard it was. "Yes. Mitchell Redford was murdered. We believe he was poisoned through a syringe then taken to a place where he was stung multiple times by wasps to cover up the hole where the poison was injected. Then his body was moved to the Red Barn, where the killer knew the car of Garrett Callis was left after he was arrested the night before after he and Mitchell Redford were in a bar fight."

My heart raced with each word I heard from Al because it was exactly what I said happened to Garrett, and the anticipation built, almost bubbling over after he moved on to Garrett's death.

"Garrett Callis has also been murdered the same way. Mr. Callis was hunted down by the killer, and in an attempt to save his own life, he tried to eat spinach to counteract the poison. We did find a similar hole to match a syringe and located the entry point where he was also poisoned by injection." As much as Al tried to be so professional, the poor guy just couldn't string together a good story without sounding like he was trying to put on a show.

None of that mattered. What mattered was we had a double murder on our hands and were no closer to finding the killer.

"We are looking for this man." I jerked up to get a good look at the wanted poster Al had concocted like an old-time Western. "This is Harrison Pierce. He is a person of interest. If you see this man, do not approach him. Please call 9-1-1 with the details of where his location is or if you've seen him. We do believe he is armed and dangerous."

My heart fell to my toes. I was about to tell Hank about Harrison asking me for help, but Al kept going.

"We do believe these two murders are tied to the cold case of Theodore Redford. We believe the past administration had held evidence and didn't consider Theodore's death a murder. We are reopening the case and will be looking at the administration led by Jerry Truman and their attempts to cover it up." Okay, so this was a bold move on Al's part since everyone in Normal loved Jerry Truman, and it took Jerry to retire in order to get a new sheriff.

"This isn't going to sit well around here." Hank kissed me. "I've got to go find Jerry. I've not seen him all day."

Hank took off before I could even give him my news about Harrison, but right now, that didn't seem so important. Agnes Swift was the most important person to see.

"Thanks, Gert!" I grabbed the coffee in exchange for some dollars and also took the bag she'd put together for the campground as I headed out the door so I could get into my car, where I was heading straight for the sheriff's department.

CHAPTER THIRTEEN

The police station was a little bit outside downtown, in the business district, right near the Cookie Crumble. The only reason Christine and her sister had the Cookie Crumble in that area of town was due to the fact that there weren't any buildings available in the downtown area.

There still weren't. Those little cottages were never available, and too bad for the cookie shop because I was sure Christine would make ten times more money with walk-in foot traffic downtown than tourists or locals having to drive to the business district to get their sugar fix.

Besides the Cookie Crumble, the white courthouse was the tallest building and right in the middle with the police station attached to it. The line of police cars told me exactly where it was located. Though it was technically a sheriff's department, I used to always waffle between the correct words of police station versus a sheriff's department.

They both did the same thing. Only, the police stations were found in the cities, and the sheriffs were in the county. Technically we could have all three, including the rangers, but for some reason, we only had the sheriff's department and rangers.

The national news vans were all lined up in the small parking lot of the department, so I had to park illegally in Al Hemmer's spot since it was vacant. No doubt in my mind he was out there looking for Jerry Truman. Which shouldn't be hard.

Jerry was a man of the law, and no matter what Al said, there was no way Jerry had done anything that wasn't on the up-and-up. I didn't care what Al thought he was going to uncover with the new reopening of Theodore's cold case.

When you walked in, there was a receptionist window and a door.

"Can I help you?" Agnes had heard the door of the station open before she saw it was me. "If you want to know about the press conference, you can go online at www.hemmersheriff and download the transcript."

I peeked through the window at the petite older woman with soft gray hair and saggy jowls. The nameplate on the other side of the glass had "Agnes" engraved across the brass.

"Well, look who's here. I've been waiting for you." She winked and jumped off her little stool behind the window.

I watched her five-foot-tall frame scurry over to the locked door between the little vestibule and the inside of the department so she could let me in.

She wore a simple button-down dress with the sheriff's logo on a tiny pocket and thick-soled white shoes.

"Is that new?" I asked when I saw the dress, because she refused to wear the ugly brown uniforms.

"Al got sick of me not listening to him. I can't wear those button pants." She patted her little belly. "And I can hardly hold it when I need to pee and trying to get that tiny button undone." She shook her head. "No way. I'm gonna wear my dress so I can yank it up when I have to go to the bathroom."

I loved and respected Agnes so much. How well Hank treated me was a direct influence from how she'd raised him. Perfectly.

"I'm assuming you're here because of Al's big news conference and not news about a wedding date?" She looked down at my ring after we'd settled down in the chair where they sat people they were booking for crimes.

"I'm sure you will know before anyone. Including Mary Elizabeth." I could see by the twinkle in her eye that my response tickled her to no end.

"Then you are here for the reports?" She gave a slight head nod toward her desk where a manilla envelope sat. "Dawn showed up here. I thought for sure she was going to ask me about you and Hank's wedding, but she didn't. She said Mitchell Redford told her he was getting death threats. Al went to Mitchell's apartment and searched high and low. Not a death threat one."

"Maybe he didn't keep them?" I questioned. "I wouldn't want them."

"Natalie said he told her he did keep them in case something happened to him. Al did tell Natalie that he'd keep in touch with her because she had to get back to her job." Agnes shrugged. "Speaking of bathroom."

I was happy to hear Natalie had left town now that the holiday was over.

Agnes eased back up from the chair she just sat down in.

"My bladder fills up so quick these days." Agnes and I both knew she didn't need to go potty but was removing herself from the area so she didn't see me take the file she'd really left for me to take on her desk.

I didn't even open the file. I slipped it into my bag just as the dispatch phone lit up. All the lines lit up.

"Agnes!" I called out of the side of my mouth, throwing my voice toward the bathroom but keeping my eyes on the multiple phone lines lighting up. "I think something is happening."

She bolted out of the bathroom and moved faster than I'd ever seen her.

"9-1-1 dispatch, what's your emergency?" she asked. "Cookie Crumble. Got it."

The other lines continued to call, in but she didn't miss a beat. She grabbed the dispatch phone.

"Attention 904B." She rattled off some codes. I didn't know what they meant, but I knew she spouted out the address of the Cookie Crumble. "All units!"

She clicked off the dispatch phone and went directly to the 9-1-1 calls.

"9-1-1 dispatch, what is your emergency?" She did this through all the calls and let them know fire trucks and deputies were on the way before she turned her attention back to me. "Mae, the Cookie Crumble is on fire."

"Fire?" I didn't even have time to get any more details from her. In fact, I don't even recall leaving the sheriff's department.

My adrenaline kicked in, and I ran to the Cookie Crumble, where the fire department had already gotten to the flames, since they were literally located right there in the business district.

I would've been relieved to see they were putting out the flames, but when one of the firefighters came running out with a person, I could tell by the cute pigtails it was Christine Watson.

CHAPTER FOURTEEN

The cold hard tile floor was so ugly and dingy. Astringent hand sanitizer, latex, soap mixed in with stagnant coffee, and bleach married together to make the unforgettable hospital smell. No matter where you visited a hospital, they all smelled the same.

Not a bit of Thanksgiving cheer was in eyeshot. Well, Dottie's red hair was sticking up all over the place, so I guessed that was a bit of color.

She was nestled between Betts and Abby in the chairs of the waiting room. Queenie had decided to burn off nervous energy by walking the halls. I stood next to the emergency room swinging door and looked through the small porthole windows to see if I could tell what was going on with Christine.

Tears stung my eyes as the reality of memories of the shooting flames coming out of Cookie Crumble started to settle, making an unwanted memory.

At first the smell of the bakery goods inside the building covered the outside air but quickly gave way to a smoky campfire smell of wood as it morphed into the chemical smell that burned the nose and throat as it mingled with the air.

"Hey, you 'k?" Dottie asked. I'd not noticed she'd come up behind me.

"No." I turned around. The dam broke. Tears fell down my cheeks. "You should've seen her lifeless body."

Lifeless body. The words hit my brain. Syringe. Poison.

I banged on the swinging doors. They weren't the kind that would open if you pushed them. Someone at the nurse's station had to buzz you in.

The little metal box buzzed to life.

"Do you need something?" The crackly voice echoed out of it.

"Poison! Christine Watson was poisoned! Give her an antidote or something." I didn't know the right words.

The door buzzed, and I grabbed the handle, opening it to run inside.

I didn't pay any attention to the Laundry Club Ladies, but when the doctor greeted me at the nurses station, Abby, Betts, and Dottie were standing behind me.

"She was passed out because of poison." I hurried my words after the doctor questioned my response. "She is part of the group of young people in Normal that recently died."

My words weren't making sense.

"Listen here, buddy." Dottie grabbed a fistful of lab coat and dragged the doctor enough for him to lean forward. "Just give her the medication for poison."

Betts put her hand on Dottie's and uncurled the fist.

"Doctor." Betts put on her sensible voice. "We believe someone injected our friend with poison. I'm not sure what kind."

"Yes. Yes we are." I'd forgotten I had the final autopsy report in the file in my bag. I pulled it out and shoved it in the doctor's chest. "You'll find a final autopsy report of another one of our friends who was also poisoned."

The doctor didn't hesitate.

"Go back to the waiting room, and I'll see what I can do." He turned to go back to Christine's little room divided by a curtain. "I think she's been poisoned."

A relief settled inside of me after I heard him tell the people behind the curtain.

The lady at the nurses station carted us right back to the waiting room, where she continued to assure us they'd let us know what was going on.

Queenie had come back with a trayful of coffee from the machine. She distributed them while Abby told her what happened with the poison theory.

"I sure hope Christine had on clean underwear." Dottie's nose curled after she took a drink of the coffee. "This is awful," she spat.

"Why on earth would you care about her underwear?" Queenie was mad, no doubt about Dottie's complaint about the coffee since she was the one who'd gotten it.

"There might be a good-lookin' doctor in there for her. She's single, and dirty underwear ain't attractive." Dottie plucked a cigarette out of her case. "Excuse me, but I've got to get the taste of lead out of my mouth."

Leave it to Dottie to still play matchmaker when someone was on their deathbed. I guessed you could look at it in a positive way and give Dottie credit for believing Christine was going to be just fine.

"Don't mind her," Abby said to Queenie as she choked down a sip of the coffee. "She's upset like us about Christine, and you know Dottie handles grief different than us."

"She's an old curmudgeon." Queenie's lip turned up. She took a drink of the coffee, her lips tugged apart. "She's right, though. This is awful coffee."

Hank came through the entrance and glanced around before he noticed us.

"How's it going?" he asked me after I'd met him halfway. "Granny called me."

"I think she was poisoned like the others." Hearing myself say it made my eyes water again.

"It's going to be okay. The doctors here are good." Hank's green eyes hugged me with kindness when I looked into them. "You okay?"

"Yeah." I nodded. "Have you heard from Jerry?"

"No. I went to his house, and Emmalyn is there. She said he left this morning and she hasn't heard from him. She said Al Hemmer stopped by. He was looking for Jerry but didn't tell her why. She'd not seen the news, so I don't think she has a clue what is going on." Hank's cheeks puffed out when he let go of a deep breath. "I hate to ask you to get involved, but do you think you could stop by and see if she knows anything? You and her get along so well, she might tell you something."

"Sure. I can do that. It'll give me a reason to leave here after I know Christine is going to be okay." I didn't have the energy to talk too much about the case. My head was only focused on Christine getting better. Staying alive.

"Christine Watson family?" A lady in scrubs appeared from a corridor.

"Here!" all of us yelled and rushed over.

"It looks like she was poisoned, but with your quick thinking, the doctors reversed the poison in time." She looked between all of us. The name on her badge read Betsy. "You saved her life. She's going to be groggy but will be okay. We are keeping her here tonight to monitor her vitals. She's comfortable right now. We want to keep her heart rhythm steady, so we aren't going to allow any visitors tonight. I'll call you in the morning with an update."

"Here's my number." I wanted her to call me, so when she had her pen at the ready, I gave her my number and name. "Do you know when she'll be discharged tomorrow?"

Unfortunately she wasn't able to even give a time or roundabout time. She said it depended on when the doctors did their rounds, but she promised she'd give me a call.

All of us stood outside in the cold, bitter weather that appeared even colder after the sun went down. We were all so grateful and made a plan to get back together at some point tomorrow. I knew I couldn't meet at the laundromat because it was my morning to work in the office.

Plus I wanted to come see Christine if I did get a free moment and possibly bring her home with me. There was no way I was going to let her go to her house with the killer on the loose.

With a plan in place, I got into my little Ford and headed over to the Trumans' to make good on my agreement with Hank to go see Emmalyn.

There weren't any cars in their driveway. I glanced around their neighborhood to check out where they lived. Not that I had any interest in moving to one of the neighborhoods on the outskirts of Normal, though they all still had gorgeous views of the Daniel Boone National Forest, but I loved living in the campground and making sure the guests were happy.

Having an owner on-site made all the difference in the world. And the guests made sure they added those to their reviews on the campground apps, as well as their social media. It was Abby who was the whiz at social, and I paid to take whatever reviews she'd found and somehow repurpose those as advertisements by using her famous hashtag skills.

But my thoughts brought me right back to the Trumans. The closed garage made me wonder if Jerry's car was in there and he was hiding out. It seemed very odd he'd suddenly disappear when the heat was on about the cold case for Theodore Redford that Al Hemmer was reopening.

Very suspicious if you asked me. Again, Jerry was innocent until proven guilty of anything. His actions were what made him stand out from the crowd and make everyone have a little inkling he might know more than he was willing to divulge back then.

I went around the side of the garage to see if there was a window to look in. If Jerry's car was there and Emmalyn told me he wasn't, I would be armed with the fact his car was there—who came to get him, or did he rent a car?

So many different directions I could take with her if I needed to. Disappointment settled when I saw there weren't any windows into the garage, which meant I had to get inside, make small talk, and get her to leave me alone where the entrance to the garage was so I could take a peek inside.

Emmalyn had decorated their landscape in the front of the house to match the season. She had a stack of pumpkins from largest to smallest in the center of some potted colorful mums along with a welcome sign made out of planks.

There was a wooden bench catty-corner at the edge of the house where she'd put a fuzzy blanket along with a couple of inviting pillows. It was inviting and cozy. All of it married to the look of fall she was going for.

I knocked on the door just below the grapevine wreath filled with dried leaves and a big wooden T in the middle that signaled the initial of Truman.

"Why, Mae West," she greeted me with a shocked look. "What a nice surprise."

"Hi, I was driving past and noticed how cute your decorations were." I looked toward the landscape. "I had to stop and tell you how much I love it."

"You almost missed them." She stood at the door, fussing with her hair as if she were trying to make it presentable. She looked fine. "I'm going to be putting out all the winter things. I told Jerry to get his butt in gear and get up in the attic to get my stuff."

"Winter?" I choked out and forced myself to have a coughing fit.

"Let me get you a glass of water." She opened the door wider for me.

"No." I wagged my hand in front of me, giving another good round of fake coughs. "You're busy. I'm fine," I choked.

"Don't be ridiculous. I'm just making my Christmas cards." She left the door wide open and disappeared into the house.

When I found her in the kitchen at the sink, she had the tap turned on and was filling up a glass. I gave a few more coughs before I took the glass. With a few sips down, I sighed.

"Thank you. I have no idea what that coughing fit was all about." I glanced around the kitchen for an entry to the garage. There were three doors.

The only one I knew for sure was the back door, because it had a window and I could see out into the backyard.

"I bet it's allergies. We might have the best views in the world around here and the best seasons, but those changes give birth to so many allergies." Her shoulders lifted to her ears before they fell back down in place.

She moved over to the table, where it looked like she was doing her cards.

"I thought you said you were doing Christmas cards, not making them." I looked at all the glitter, markers, and glue along with the piece of paper.

"I make every card I send out." She smiled. "This year Jerry put you on Hank's card." She threw her hands in the air. "Which reminds me."

She batted around the table, moving various things around until she uncovered an address book.

"I need to know your lot number at the campground because I'm going to make you a special card with my new glitter." She handed me the address book and ink pen. Then she picked up a bottle of red glitter.

It didn't look too fancy to me, but when she tapped some out on a piece of white construction paper, there was a shimmer of gold.

"This is very expensive stuff, and they don't give you a whole lot." She frowned. "Packaging nowadays is deceiving. I thought I was getting a whole jar, but when I opened the lid this morning, this was what was in it."

"Same with potato chips." I snickered and quickly wrote my address in her book. I glanced around the kitchen to figure out what wasn't in there so I could ask for it and get her to leave me alone to check out these doors.

"Where's Jerry?" I asked.

"I have no idea. Hank came by looking for him too. I've called him a couple of times but nothing." She didn't seem to be concerned. "It never fails how he runs into someone and they get talking. Jerry has always had the gift of gab."

"Do you have any lotion?" I wrung my hands together. "They seem awfully dry. I bet these allergies you're talking about has made my hands dry."

"Of course." Her eyes darted around the kitchen. "I have to go grab some out of my bathroom."

She muttered some more things as she left the kitchen, but I didn't hear a thing she said. I moved quickly, opening up the first closed door. It was a pantry.

The second door was the gold mine. I stuck my head through the door and saw Emmalyn's car. Not Jerry's, so I guessed what she said about him not being home was honest.

"Here you go." She was looking down at the bottle, and when she saw my big head in the garage, caught red-handed, she asked, "Are you looking for a bathroom?"

"No. Actually—" For a split second, I was going to tell her the truth, but shifted. "I was looking at your house, and I love the layout. Hank and I have been talking about where we are going to live."

"Jerry told me Hank said you'll be living at Happy Trails." She made me smile.

I loved how Hank talked about our future to his buddy.

"Yes, but when I look to see what you have here, I have to wonder if it's the best thing." I shut the door. "Plus I bet it's nice to have a warm car to jump into and go during the winters." I took the lotion from her and pumped out a couple of squirts. "I have to go outside and start my little jalopy to get the heater going so I can brush off the snow."

"That makes me cold thinking of it." She shivered in a joking manner. "Some advice from an old married woman?"

I nodded. "Of course."

"Sometimes we don't ask for unsolicited advice. I thought I'd ask, but just be married. Who cares where you live. Enjoy yourselves as a couple, and you will marry with each other. Like the word married. Two people coming together to make one life. No different than we marry ingredients to make the perfect recipe. Sometimes we throw in things that don't taste good, so it doesn't marry into the recipe well." She made a good analogy. "What I'm saying is there's no hurry, but if you really are looking, I hear June and Bob next door are looking to sell in the spring. They even have a pool."

She walked over to the back door and pointed to the house next door. I glanced over her shoulder, feeling a little bad about the lie I'd just told her.

"I guess I better go. I don't want to take up any more of your time since you are getting your cards ready." I was afraid if I stayed too long, I'd open my big mouth and tell her how I felt like Jerry was on the run.

Then if he wasn't, I sure would make a big mess of a friendship between the four of us.

"Do you want to make a card?" she offered.

I declined and got out of there.

She waved me off, and I put the car in gear, looking out the back window as I backed up.

Jerry Truman had put the nose of his car in the driveway and put his car in gear when he saw I was coming out.

I looked out the front window of my car and noticed he'd put up the automatic garage door. This was my moment. I shoved my car in park and turned off the ignition, getting out of the car so he knew I was staying.

He pulled his car up to the curb and got out, where I greeted him.

"Hey, Mae." He looked confused. "What are you doing here?"

"That's no way to treat a guest!" Emmalyn scolded him from the front door.

"I wanted to ask you a few questions about Theo Redford's death." I watched as his eyes slowly blinked as if he knew this was going to happen sooner or later. Maybe not questioned by me but by someone.

"Emmalyn, I'll be inside in a few. I want to talk to Mae about Hank's bachelor party." He made it look so effortless to lie to her.

"Come back, Mae!" she called before she went back inside and shut the door.

He leaned against his car and folded his arms across his chest.

"I figured this would come back to bite me one day." He stared at me.

"What do you mean?" I wondered.

"Varney Gould was the coroner when Theo died. He felt like Theo didn't die from a fall. He said the way Theo landed, the way the soil wasn't disturbed when someone would fall... nor did the injuries fit with how someone would look after a long fall like that." He looked off. "When he told me he found drugs in his system, I didn't want the community alarmed. Drugs had started to become rampant around here during that time. We found all sorts of hikers, tourists dead from overdoses. I didn't want the word to get around that we let people hike, do drugs in the woods. A free-for-all for drug abusers."

There was pain in the tone of his voice.

"We were in an economic decline and struggling to make the shops stay open. Put food on people's tables. As the sheriff, I needed to find a way to keep the townsfolk safe, and saying we had a drug problem in the area wasn't the way to do it. So I did the next best thing I could, try to get Rex Rivera to shut down the liquor store." He frowned. "Everyone knew the kids around here drank and went into the forest, but where were their parents? That's when we decided to do the big push for the underage drinking campaign at the schools."

"How did that turn out?" I asked.

"It took the spotlight off the drug part of Theo's death." He uncurled his arms and pushed off the car to stand. "The thought of Theo being pushed or drugged just went away, and I left it there. It's something that's haunted me for years. I've tried to push away any sort of talk when people bring it up, and I feared someone was going to sue me and take everything Emmalyn and I'd built here."

The fear of losing everything was a great motive to kill, and his story only told me he probably knew more than he was telling me.

"Will Varney say anything now that two more are dead from that group and Al reopened the cold case?" I asked.

"Varney died years ago and took the secret with him. I was hoping this would never come back to light, but here we are." His tone shifted. His eyes bored into me.

A lump formed in my throat.

"I better go. I have to relieve Dottie at the office." I pinched a nervous grin. "Hank's been looking for you. I'll let him know you're home."

"You don't need to do that. I'll call him myself." He stood there, watching me leave.

I gave him one last glance in the rearview mirror as I drove away.

He'd not moved an inch, but I did notice his mouth was clenched tighter, and his hands were fisted.

CHAPTER FIFTEEN

Dottie was raring to go when I got there. She mentioned something about her soap opera and needing to catch up, so if I needed her for the campground or there was a break in the murder cases to come find her in her camper.

Dottie was so great about letting Fifi hang out with her. She'd even put Fifi's fall coat on her, since the sweet baby would shiver in any temperature lower than seventy degrees. Most of the time Chester went with Hank for the day, so we didn't have to worry about him needing to be let out or socialized unless Hank otherwise asked me to check on Chester.

"Let's go for a walk," I called to Fifi, waking her from the comfort of her little bed Dottie had placed next to her desk.

Fifi jumped to her feet, happily clicking her nails on the old office floor tiles.

"I wish I would wake up that happy every day." I didn't bother putting her leash on since it was daylight.

I still hadn't felt that feeling of the season, and I embraced the days as they got darker earlier. Though it was in the middle of the day, the sun was already starting to head down the other side of the mountain.

It would be dark before 6:00 p.m., and I was happy to see most of the campground guests were already back from their day out.

"Good afternoon," I greeted a guest in one of the bungalows after Fifi had went up to them first. "Do you need anything?"

"I wanted to see if I could purchase one of the coffee baskets," he asked. "My wife loves the coffee served in the hospitality room, and when we went to the Trails Coffee Shop, Gert, the owner, told us you sold baskets with products from the shop."

"Actually." I was so pleased to hear he and his wife loved the coffee so much they went to the coffee shop. That told me my idea of cross-promotions between me and the other shops were working. "I got a new batch of fresh coffees from her this morning. I'll make up a quick basket and bring it down."

"Great." He glanced back when we heard his wife walking around from the back of the bungalow. "I want to surprise her, so just put it on my tab. I'm taking her to dinner tonight, so do you mind putting it inside?"

"No problem." I knew I could do better than that. I'd have some other extra goodies for them, on the house, but he didn't need to know that.

It was these extra little touches that made the guests love Happy Trails Campground enough to come back several times as well as spread the word.

"Have a good night," I told them both and clicked my tongue. "Fifi, leave this nice couple to enjoy themselves."

Fifi and I made our way around the lake, taking a minute to stand on the pier to make sure the lake looked healthy going into the winter months. From what I could see from one of the other guests with a line in the water, the fish must've gone deeper already. His bobber looked like it was positioned on the line to fall deeper into the water.

Satisfied the campground was good for the rest of the night, Fifi and I made our way back up to the office so I could get the baskets ready.

I had to taste the freshly ground coffee in order to really sell it, right? At least that was what I told myself when I opened one of the bags and made a fresh pot of coffee in the office coffee maker.

A hint of pumpkin and caramel floated through the office as the carafe filled. I pulled out five baskets from the office closet and started to fill them up. Each got a bag of Gert's special-blend coffee, a mug with the Happy Trails Campground logo, and a couple of seasonal cookies that were from the Cookie Crumble and individually wrapped.

I held one of the cookies in my hand and couldn't help but think about Christine and what on earth would become of the bakery.

My attention shifted to the investigation and the wipe-off board hanging on the wall near Dottie's desk with all the campground activities listed on it, so when guests came into the office, it was staring them in the face.

"What do we have, Fifi?" I asked her, and when I walked past Dottie's desk to go to the whiteboard, I took a dog biscuit out of the jar and handed it to her.

The eraser glided over the written words on the board with each stroke, soon to be replaced with suspect names and motives.

I could easily just take out the sleuthing notebook where Abby had written all the things down, but when I wrote things for myself and went over them in my head, sometimes little clues that didn't seem like good leads would create a puzzle to take us down another path.

I still wrote down Harrison's name. His dad gave the alcohol to all his friends and the Rivera boy. His lifestyle was altered because his father was not only sued but went broke. That would bring on a lot of anger, and when he came back for the reunion the night before Thanksgiving, things were triggered.

Also the thought of what truly happened the day on the trail a long time ago with Theodore Redford seemed to be something all of them wanted to keep a secret.

What about Mr. Rivera? He was angry and sued. One by one he was plucking them off to get revenge on them for being the gateway to his son's alcohol poisoning, which from what I understood, left his son with some brain damage.

I stood back and looked at the board. Clearly I had to go see the Riveras and get their take on things now that Al had reopened the cold case that was taking place the same time the Riveras' case had happened.

Too bad Rex was dead. He might've been able to give some answers.

The coffeepot beeped that it was brewed. I walked over and got my mug off my desk so I could fill it up.

With my mug in my grip, I slowly sipped the coffee and stared through the steam at the board.

I walked over and wrote down Jerry Truman. It literally pained me to do so. The thought of what could be the truth to such a nice man was what an ugly and festering secret could do to a person.

Drive them to kill to keep any sort of secret buried.

That secret was buried with Varney, the coroner at the time, as well as Theo Redford. The only other person who truly knew what happened was Mitchell Redford, who blamed Garrett Callis, now both dead along with what they knew.

I circled Mitchell's name before I wrote down "death threats" and came back to what Dawn Gentry had told me.

I put the lid back on the dry-erase marker and walked over to pick up my phone.

"Hey, Dawn." I called her with an idea. "I know you said you and Mitchell Redford were friends."

There was an inkling in my bones that they were more than just friends.

"And I want to help find out his killer. I need to get into his apartment." I told her about how Agnes said she'd gone to the sheriff to tell them about the death threat notes, but they couldn't find them.

"We weren't dating yet, but we spent a lot of time together," she said, her tone quieter than normal. "There was a good chance we wouldn't have been more than friends."

"I'm sorry. But I'm committed to finding out who did this." I left out the part where Harrison had asked me to help. "I think this stems from his cousin Theodore's case."

"I think so too." And that was all she needed to say for me and her to make a plan for me to pick her up tomorrow and take a trip to Mitchell's apartment even though she said she didn't have a key.

CHAPTER SIXTEEN

T he wind was howling the next morning. Just the sheer sound told me it was going to be a blustery day even though the sun was brilliantly shining the morning dew away as it gave a spotlight to the earthy, rust-colored backdrop of the mountains.

It was one of those perfect hiking days where you'd bundle up and be able to keep your layers on due to the fact that the sun wasn't going to warm you to take them off.

These were the days hikers seemed to love and loved to visit the forest. The die-hard camping fans.

I'd have loved to hike the Red Fox Trail to the stream and back. It was a quick trail where the mouth started right behind the tiki hut, but I had to open the office.

Fifi didn't like the cold mornings, so she stayed tucked in bed while I got ready and headed down to the office to check on any overnight messages.

The whiteboard glared at me when I hit the lights on. I was happy to see my good night's sleep didn't change my mind about going to Mitchell's apartment.

"Morning!" Henry came in the office. He had on his thick coveralls that he wore outside during the colder months. He grinned. His big nose spread across his face as his smile widened, exposing his missing two front teeth. The scraggly ends of his hair poked out from underneath the edges of his baseball cap.

"Hey!" I was happy to see him. "What's the word in the campground?"

Henry took the lid off his thermal mug and filled it up with coffee.

"I've got to replace some firewood in bungalow two and five. The couple of rental campers need the toilets looked at." He put the lid back on. Small puffs of steam escaped from the hole in the top. "I think they bought regular toilet paper."

"I put in several septic rolls." I rolled my eyes.

No matter how many times I posted the signs in campers' bathrooms about how we can't use regular toilet paper in the campers not only because of the septic but because when regular toilet paper expanded in the campers' sewage lines, they clogged up the camper, and it wasn't a good thing, not to mention the sewer backup smell.

"I'm gonna have to unclog one of them." His nose curled, and the corners of his lips dipped down.

"Do you mind keeping an eye on the office this morning?" I didn't want to ask Dottie. She'd been working hard, and she must've needed some sleep because there still weren't any lights on in her camper, and she'd yet to come out to smoke.

A sure sign she wasn't up.

"I need to go see Dawn Gentry." I saw his eyes move over my head to the whiteboard.

"Mmhmm." His disapproving hum wasn't necessary but apparent. "I'll keep an eye on 'er."

"Thanks. It'll be a couple of hours." That would give me enough time to get some paperwork done as well as make sure he got a good start on the plumbing issues in the rental campers.

Before I knew it, Fifi was nestled back in our camper, I phoned to say good morning to Hank, and Dawn Gentry was in my car, giving me directions to Mitchell Redford's apartment.

"How on earth do you think we are going to get in?" Dawn pointed to the second-story balcony off Mitchell's apartment.

We stood on the sidewalk, looking up.

"What about the lady at the office? Did Mitchell ever have you down as a contact?" I wondered with a shot in the dark.

My aim wasn't too bad.

"I am on his emergency contacts. We got locked out one night, and the office suggested he put someone on just in case he ever needed a key," she said and darted off before she finished talking.

She told me about that night and how they'd decided to jump on their motorcycles to get ice cream. He rode on the back of her motorcycle and left his keys in the apartment. The locks on the door were the kind that locked behind you, and that was when they had to call maintenance to let them in.

"Can I help you?" There was a woman sitting in a glass office when we entered the community building.

"Wow, this place is nice." The open area with the floor-to-ceiling fireplace with the three small couches gathered around it and a large table with eight chairs around it were set for a Thanksgiving feast with fancy china and a nice centerpiece.

"We offer it for guests to rent for special occasions." The lady pointed to the back. "There's a kitchen back there for cooking. Some of our guests only have one-bedroom apartments and want to host their larger families for holidays. Are you looking to rent?"

"No. I'm Dawn Gentry, and a friend of mine, Mitchell Redford, rents here." As Dawn talked, I could see the woman stiffen. "I'm on his list of contacts."

"By your reaction, I can see you know what's happened to Mitchell." I had to point it out.

"Yes. I'm sorry for your loss. The sheriff was here yesterday, and they had a warrant to go through his things." She looked at Dawn. "Do you have your ID on you?"

"I do." She unzipped the small breast pocket on her moto leather jacket to retrieve her license.

The woman took it, and once she was satisfied with the name, she handed it back.

"I don't need to check the records, because the sheriff took his rental file, so I did look at Mitchell's contact list in case someone came in." She opened a drawer in her desk and shuffled through what sounded like keys. "You and one other person were listed."

"Really?" Dawn drew back.

"Yes. Ryan Rivera," she told us without any coaxing.

I tried not to give off *OMG* shocked body language until Dawn and I got the key and were safely out of the eyes of the office woman.

"Did you hear that?" I muttered like a ventriloquist as we walked back down to the apartment building Mitchell lived in.

"Who is that? He never mentioned anyone to me." Dawn seemed shocked to not know this.

"Long story longer," I teased, letting her know the details of what I knew were going to take a hot minute to explain.

While I did my best to explain how the Riveras connected with the death of Theodore Redford as well as Garrett and Mitchell, the connection made for a story Mitchell had told her.

"Oh gosh. I told you he told me about his cousin. He also told me about this other kid who they gave liquor to when they were hanging around Harrison's dad's liquor store." She was searching through the drawers in the kitchen while I was lifting up the couch cushions, though I could tell by the wonky way they weren't exactly fitting in the couch that the sheriff had already searched there.

I found that when people were so focused on searching for one thing, they might miss what was in front of them, so I didn't mind searching again.

There was a wire basket filled with what looked like birthday cards hanging on the side of one upper kitchen cabinet that was on the end.

"He never said he was in touch with the family still." She sounded a little wounded, which told me she and Mitchell were much closer than she'd let on.

Dawn was that way. She was fairly private, and though the Laundry

Club Ladies and I made her an honorary member, she never came to anything.

"Did he have a birthday recently?" I asked and took the cards out to see what everyone said to him. "I love birthday cards…" I opened the first one and realized it was no birthday card.

"His birthday is in the summer. He always talked about summer camping near one of the lakes hidden off a trail around here." She walked over and peeked at the card. "What is it?"

"It's handmade death threats." One after the other, I opened each one of them. "Al didn't find them because he probably thought they were birthday cards like I thought."

The outside of them said different things like happy birthday, hello, thinking of you, like the generic box cards you'd purchase for all occasions at a big box store. Only, these were handmade.

"Keep your mouth shut or else," I read the inside of the next one that was written in dried red glitter with golden flakes. "Dawn," I gasped and held the card to my chest. "I've seen this glitter before."

"Where?" she asked with big, wide-open eyes.

The look in her eyes told me if she knew where I'd seen the glitter, she'd immediately go to Al, and that was something I wasn't quite ready to do. In fact, it was the opposite.

Jerry and Emmalyn Truman were very close to Hank. So close that I was sure Hank was going to ask Jerry to be his best man in our wedding.

Emmalyn didn't look like a killer. Which was also a good cover for her to be the killer. The glitter did point to her, and she did say it was very special glitter. Did she make the comment to me about how the glitter wasn't filled to the top when she opened it, trying to cover her tracks if someone, me, linked the death threats to her Christmas cards?

The fact remained that a woman will do anything to keep her man safe, especially a man who has a very dark secret. It was entirely possible Jerry had no idea Emmalyn had sent Mitchell the threats.

I for sure had to use kid gloves with this one, and that was why I decided not to tell Dawn who I thought it was.

"Let me look into it more." I closed all of the death threat cards and piled them up. "Why don't you take these for safekeeping? Don't tell Al just yet. Let me follow the clue to see if my hunch was right. I'll be over at the Milkery this afternoon to let you know what I find out."

CHAPTER SEVENTEEN

Dawn Gentry hemmed and hawed around about my plan to investigate things. For an instant, I almost took the cards from her for fear she'd do the thing I'd asked her not to do.

Take them to Al.

I was willing to give her the benefit of the doubt and wait to see what I found out. There were two more people on my list to see whose names had floated around since the murders now and then.

Ryan and Carson Rivera.

The father and son.

I wanted to see what they knew about Jerry Truman's involvement when Theodore Redford had died. Jerry was the only link to all three murders. Emmalyn did say the night of the reunion at the Red Barn Restaurant how awful that time in her life was and how she never wanted to revisit it again.

Was this her way of making sure it didn't surface?

I gripped the wheel as I zoomed out of the Milkery with the GPS on my phone directly leading me to Red Hill Pines, the road where Ryan Rivera lived. I didn't know where Maria lived and waited on Abby to get me the information.

She was working at the library today, and they were always hosting events during the holidays, which made Abby pretty much scarce from the Laundry Club Ladies.

Luckily the uncharted mountain roads were cleared by the transportation road crew and weren't slick from the light snowfall. Still, I took my time and tried to think ahead about what I was going to say to Ryan.

I took a second to gather my thoughts when I pulled up to the very odd home that'd been a marvel for everyone who passed by it.

Like everyone had mentioned, it was built by an architect, and it was literally half on the earth and half dangling over the cliffside. All the walls were glass, and there couldn't be a bad view of the Daniel Boone National Forest from anywhere inside.

My mouth salivated at the idea of them giving me a tour. I'd even planned out asking for one, then Carson opened the door.

In a wheelchair, making me lose all sense of thought and conversation I'd planned to say.

"You're Carson." I almost didn't expect to see a bright-looking young man who had sustained a brain injury due to drinking too much alcohol that sent him into a coma.

"I am. And you are?" The dark-haired, good-looking young man sent a smile that brightened my insides, shoving past the dreary reason I was there. "Ma'am?"

"Goodness. Ma'am." I laughed due to the fact he probably wasn't much younger than me.

"Can we help you?" A much older version of Carson appeared behind him.

"Are you Ryan Rivera?" I didn't even need to ask. The resemblance was uncanny. If it weren't for the trickling of a few gray hairs, they'd pass as twins. "Of course you are."

I cleared my throat and gave a quick shake of my head to get me back in the game.

"I'm sorry to bother the two of you." The judgment I'd put on of what I thought Carson was going to be like hit me hard and made me sad to even think the worst of his condition. When in fact, he looked great. "My name is Mae West. I am here because I'm helping to investigate the murders of Garrett Callis and Mitchell Redford."

Investigate might've been pushing it a bit.

"What do you want us for?" Carson asked. His gloved hands were on the wheels of his sporty-looking wheelchair.

"I think their murder has to do with you. Not directly but with Theodore Redford's cold case that we've opened." Technically it wasn't *we* so much as the sheriff, but it was all in the semantics, right?

If they chose to open up to me about it without asking me for my credentials, there was no problem, right?

Ryan stepped out from behind his son and walked out onto the small concrete-slab porch.

"I'll talk to her, son," he told Carson.

"No, Dad. I can talk to her too." Carson wheeled himself out onto the porch and down the ramp to where I was standing.

"Then we will all talk out here." Ryan didn't want me in the home, and I think Carson knew it, so that was why they'd all come out.

"The truth of the matter is my father hasn't accepted what happened to me as a good thing." Carson glanced back at his dad. There was a stone-cold hardness to Ryan's jaw. "I have no hard feelings toward Mr. Pierce. I know my dad sued them and ran them out of business, but it wouldn't've given me the full life I've had. A gift of God."

His father harrumphed.

"My dad would never admit it, but I was headed down a very wrong path back them. Even though I was a kid, I had no purpose in life but to get in trouble. Mom and Dad were already on the brink of a divorce. We still didn't have money, and I did everything illegally I could to get my hands on anything that would make me numb." Carson's words were so sincere and touched my heart.

And I understood exactly what he was saying and where he was going with this concept of the hand he'd been dealt.

"It's made my life full. I've traveled all over the country, speaking to high school students, educating them on the effects of alcohol and letting them see what it did to me. I am glad Mr. Pierce gave it to me, and I'm glad I had brain damage that affected my ability to walk." He patted his legs.

"How did it affect your walking?" I was thinking his spine, not the brain.

"Binging the alcohol brought on a stroke among other things, and that part of my brain is damaged. The rest of me is all good." He flashed that smile. "And Mitchell Redford and Harrison Pierce have gone out of their way to help me over the years."

"I think you've answered all her questions, son." Ryan stepped off the porch and put his hand on his son's shoulder.

"They helped you?" I wondered.

"They have been great getting my foot into the door of various organizations and even donating to my foundation. They even partnered with me on a few events." He nodded. "When I heard what happened to Mitchell, I couldn't believe it."

"And we want no part of it. My son has suffered enough from being around that group of boys," Ryan said through gritted teeth.

"I'm sorry." I felt like I needed to apologize because I could feel his hurt radiating off of him.

My phone rang in my jacket pocket, and I didn't bother looking at it. It could wait.

"Can I ask one more question?" I looked between them. When they didn't stop me, I continued, "Jerry Truman was the sheriff back then. Did you do anything to—" I started to say.

"You mean he didn't do his job properly?" Carson asked.

"Right? The case has been reopened and—"

This time Ryan interrupted me.

"You wanted to see if I killed those boys out of revenge for providing Carson the alcohol?" Ryan didn't let anything slip past him.

"I'm just looking for answers, and serious allegations are being stacked up against the former sheriff. We are just going through the files, which is what happens when a cold case is reopened." I was talking about Theodore's case and kinda proud of myself because I sounded like I knew what I was talking about.

I silenced the phone when it started to ring again. I didn't look to see who was calling.

"I didn't want revenge for the way the sheriff took care of Carson's case. We dealt with what we got and couldn't change it, so however he handled it was the way it was going to go. The only thing we had Rex Harrison pay for was any expenses insurance didn't pay for, and from the money the liquor store was cranking in, there was no reason he should've shut down." Ryan had a lot to say.

The dried leaves pushed up against the house as the wind picked up. Off in the distance the leaves were dropping so fast off the trees, it looked like warm and cozy hues of glitter were being sprinkled from the sky.

"Carson, you need to go inside. The last thing we need is for you to get pneumonia." Ryan had pretty much told me everything I needed to know for them not to be suspects in my book.

"Thank you for your time." I looked at Carson before I turned to go back to my car. "Say—" I turned around right as Carson had gotten to the door, his father behind him. "I own Happy Trails Campground, and we are hosting Thanksgiving supper in a couple of days for the community. I'd love to see you there. I think you'd make some great contacts."

"We'll see." Ryan threw a chin.

"Harrison should be there." That was yet another lie, but I was going to invite him. "And Christine Watson."

"What about Richard?" Carson asked.

"Richard?" I hadn't heard of Richard.

"Harrison, Richard, and Christine are the only ones left of that little group of six." Carson gave me a name I'd not yet heard. "Richard Denning."

The only Denning I knew of was Will Denning from the running group. He was younger and a cousin to the Redfords, but it didn't mean he didn't have an older brother.

My phone rang again.

"You better get that. Someone's trying to get in touch with you."

Carson wheeled into the house with his father closing the door behind them.

"Hello?" I asked when I'd not recognized the phone number.

"This is Betsy, the nurse from the hospital. We've been trying to call you." The woman's voice I'd recognized came through the phone.

"Hi. Is Christine ready to come be picked up?" I asked.

"That's why I was trying to get in touch with you. A man came to pick her up, and I told them you were going to, but he insisted." As she talked, panic welled up in my throat.

"Do you have a name?" I asked as calmly as I could and hurried to my car.

"I think she called him Jerry."

A quick and disturbing thought of Jerry Truman taking out each member of this group was his plan, and I had to get to Christine's house to stop him.

CHAPTER EIGHTEEN

I t took forever for my phone to hook to my car's speakers so I could keep my hands on the wheel while I drove as fast as I could without skidding off the side of the cliff on my way to Christine's house.

"Hank, really." I had tried to convince him to hunt down Jerry or head straight over to Christine's house.

"I'm telling you, Jerry isn't involved." Hank was convinced. "He told me he was going to go see Christine to see if she had any information on the fire, because Al has snuffed him and me out of any sort of investigation."

"I understand he went to pick her up, but she's not answering her phone. I tried when I left the Riveras." I continued to try to swallow the lump that was still sitting in my throat.

I was concentrating more on that than the nauseous feeling in my gut.

"I'm guessing she was getting discharged when he got there and offered her a ride. She wouldn't've left with him if she thought she was in danger." Hank made me feel like I was ridiculous.

"Of course she trusts him. He's the ex-sheriff." I cleared my throat. My eyes watered. "I know either he killed Mitchell or Emmalyn did."

"Maybelline." My name came out of his mouth sounding like a

parent scolding a child. It raked across me like nails on a chalkboard. "I can't even begin to think why you'd even say that. You know he's one of my best friends."

"I'm sure every other murderer had a best friend, but it doesn't mean they aren't killers," I blurted out then said, "I went to see Emmalyn like you asked me to. She was making Christmas cards."

"She does that every year," he said, making sure he defended them to me.

"She showed me a special glitter, and she showed me how it was only three quarters of the way full. She made sure she pointed out to me that was the way she'd gotten it." I held the little car's wheels close to the edge of the line as I made the last big curve that would send me into a straightaway and close to Christine's house.

I picked up the speed.

"I picked up Dawn Gentry, and we went into Mitchell's apartment, where I found the glitter used on a death threat." The lump in my throat was gone but was replaced by my very sweaty hands.

"Mae." Hank sounded as if he were trying to come up with something to say that would comfort me more than shame me for thinking along the lines.

"Don't Mae me." I demanded for him to take me seriously. "If he didn't kill him, then Emmalyn did. She said the other night at the Milkery on Thanksgiving how she never wanted to revisit it again. Thanks to Al Hemmer, the entire town is. Who is Richard Denning?"

"I guess one of the Dennings. They have a billion relatives." He wasn't any help.

"I'm on my way to Christine's, and I'll let you know if Jerry is there and killing Christine." I had gone a little salty on him. My call beeped in my phone. "I'm on my car speaker, so I can't see who is calling."

"Maybe it's Christine. You better get it then call me back." Hank barely got out the words before I clicked over.

"Hello? Christine?" It had to be her.

"Nope. Harrison." Hearing his deep voice made my stomach turn even more. "Any news on the case?"

"Who is Richard Denning?" I asked because I knew he'd know.

"Richard." He laughed. "You mean little weaselly Will Denning?"

"Will Denning?" It felt as if time stood still. My car was moving, and it was like it was on autopilot to Christine's house, but my mind had taken off in a totally different direction.

"Yeah. He's a cousin to the Redfords. We called him weaselly back then because he was a little weasel. Always trying to hang out with us." There was silence.

"Harrison?" I spouted off.

"Yeah." he said.

"I thought I dropped the call." I had an awful feeling.

The more memories I got, the faster my car seemed to move.

"He was there the day Theodore fell, wasn't he?" I asked.

"Yeah. You know I think the sheriff didn't interview him because his family said he was too young or something." Harrison recalled him being there. "I totally forgot about that kid. Man now. Did you see how much he's changed?"

"Harrison, I think Will Denning killed Theodore, Mitchell, and Garrett." My mouth was dry as I recalled all the events leading up to all the murders. "He said he wanted to hang out with you guys and hated how y'all treated Christine. He knew Theo was allergic to wasps, and Mitchell. He knew how to give the EpiPen shots because his whole family was given the directions from their mom just like she did with your group."

The zooming car driving past me made me jump out of my thoughts.

"He's a physical therapist in one of the nursing homes and would have access to morphine, which I bet was the drug he injected them with to overdose. So no amount of spinach was going to save Garrett." I jerked a right down Christine's street and was actually happy to see Jerry's car was there, and so was Lester's.

"Do me a favor," I told him. "Please call Al Hemmer and let him know this information."

I hit the off button and threw my car in park, tossing the keys in the passenger seat before I got out.

I had to get inside. Tell Jerry and Lester what I'd found out.

It was all making so much sense now.

From the trail we had run on where I found Theo's memorial, all the way to Will seeing the old gang at the reunion, as well as Will keeping Christine by his side with this whole running act.

I knocked on the door, and no one answered. With a heavy hand, I beat on it again. Nothing.

"They might be getting her settled into her bed." I gave them the benefit of the doubt and tried the door handle.

It wasn't a shock when the door opened. We rarely locked our doors around here. So I didn't think anything of it until I walked in and someone jumped out from behind the door and strong-armed me down to the ground.

CHAPTER NINETEEN

"Let me go!" I screamed at whoever had my hands knotted up behind my back. I flailed, but they were too strong.

When I tried to look back at them, they shifted the opposite way, pushing me toward a closed door.

"I swear you better let me go! Hank is on his way, and he's already called Al!" I felt my hands shift into one hand before they opened the closed door in front of us then shoved me in the dark room, shutting the door behind.

I felt my way around to see if I could find any windows to let light in, and when I came to a pair of legs, I gritted my teeth in hopes not to scream.

"Please tell me you're alive." I felt up to the person's chest, and there was some shallow breathing. I moved my hands up to their face and could feel it was a man's short hair, but I was not sure if it was Lester or Jerry or Will.

At this point I had no idea who was in here with me until there was some mumbling coming from the darkness.

"Who's in here?" I listened. "Use anything you have to knock on the floor so I can find you."

There was a light tapping. My head darted left to right to see if I could find the direction. I got on my hands and knees and had to crawl over whoever's body I found.

"Keep tapping. I'm coming." The moaning got closer and closer as I kept moving forward. "Where are you?" I reached my arm out in front of me as far as it would go and felt around until I hit gold. "There you are."

I saddled up to the person and used my hands to feel around their face.

"Christine," I gasped when I felt the two braided pigtails. I moved my hand to her mouth, where there was a gag in. "Hold still," I told her as she wiggled. "I'll get it off."

What seemed like forever but probably wasn't, I finally got to the back of her head, where the killer had tied it snug.

She gasped for air when I got her free.

"My hands and legs are tied." Her body wiggled and moved as if she were in a panic, which we were, but no good it would do us.

The darkness wasn't getting any lighter the longer we were in there.

"Will." She only confirmed my suspicions. "He's injected Lester and Jerry."

Time was of the essence, and trying to untie her hands would be my first thing to do since she could undo her own legs.

"Where are we in your house?" I asked her.

"My media room. There's no windows." That wasn't helpful. "He took my phone, so I can't call or use the flashlight, but there's a panel on the wall next to the television. You can use it to find the switch for the running lights around the room."

She gave me directions on which way to go in the dark. When I made it over to the wall she had directed me to, I ran my hand up along the wall to find the panel.

"Open the door, and it's the third switch down," she instructed me.

"I thought it was awfully quiet in here." Will opened the door, blinding me from the sudden light the outside was letting into the room.

There was a syringe in his hand, and since I knew he'd cared way too much for Christine, it had to be for me.

"Will, don't do this," Christine begged.

"It's all for you. Everything I've done is for you." He pawned it off like it was her fault he had to kill the three men. "Lester was going to rat me out. So I had to get rid of him. I mean, after he went to jail, I was so happy. I knew my secret would die with him. He deserves to die for killing people."

"What about you?" I was on borrowed time, so I might as well just say what I thought. "You are killing innocent people because why? They called you a weasel? They treated Christine like one of the guys? Are you keeping the lights off because it's the weasel's way out to get me in the dark so you don't have to man up and do it while looking in my eyes?"

I flipped the toggle in the panel so the lights came on, and he had to come in the room if he wanted to shut them off.

"They didn't respect her. The day on the trail when they were all hiking and making me lag behind, I overheard them talking about her in a way that wasn't appropriate for a girl. The disrespect they had made me sick. When Theo got stung, he told the others to go ahead of him." His eyes shifted to Christine. "I knew I had to protect you from Mitchell. He bent down into his backpack, and when he realized he had mine, he told me to get his EpiPen from it."

The crazy evil grin grew on Will's face.

"He did the little-kid-gimme hand. He said, 'I'm going to die if you don't give me it,' right before he clutched his throat. His eyes had a look of terror, and he stumbled backward." Will shrugged. He moved his gaze down to Jerry.

I could see by the movement in Jerry's chest he was still breathing. Shallow but still alive.

"Technically I didn't kill Theo. I just didn't help him. The group sorta broke up after that. But Christine and I remained friends, and I knew one day we'd be together even though I was a little younger." The look he gave her was so unnerving.

"You can't possibly think you can get away with this?" I asked. "Tell him, Christine. He set your place on fire."

"Yes. I did. I had to teach her a lesson in not to reject me. I'm the one who made the call to 9-1-1 so they'd save her," he said in a low voice.

"What?" Christine spit out. "You have ruined my life. My bakery!"

"No. I made you realize the rejection you gave me the other day had to have consequences." I had no idea what he was talking about. "And now that she is here, I can get rid of her so you don't have the excuse that you need to run with her. You'll be back up on your feet and running with me every day like we used to."

"What planet are you living on?" I grunted out with a snort. "Do you really think you're going to get away with killing two or possibly five people?" I lifted my hand and counted them off in hopes to thoroughly confuse him and buy me some time to get me, Christine, and Jerry out of here safely. "Let's see, there's Mitchell, Garrett, oh, Theo." I plucked each finger in the air. "Then there's me and Jerry."

"Don't forget Lester. He's in the other room. I had a bit of a confession before I stuck him." He lifted his little syringe in the air. "None of this will matter soon."

"Christine!" Harrison called out from the family room. "Where are you?"

"In here!" she screamed without warning him of Will.

"With Richard Denning! The weasel!" I hollered back. "You're gonna get it now!"

Will jerked around, looking about as though he were searching for an escape, but when he realized the only way out was the door he was standing by, he lifted his arm up in the air and ran toward Harrison, his finger on the tip of the plunger, ready to push it down as soon as the needle went into Harrison.

Harrison pulled his hand from behind his back and shoved one of Christine's couch pillows he must've grabbed on his way down to find us, knocking Will to the ground. The syringe skittered across the floor.

"The shot thingy!" Christine screamed and ran out of the room to go after the syringe as Harrison knotted up Will's gangly limbs.

"Still the little weasel." Harrison snickered before he ordered us to call 9-1-1.

CHAPTER TWENTY

Happy Trails Campground looked like someone had flown over it in an airplane and dumped all of the Macy's Thanksgiving Day parade floats on it. A few days had gone by since my near-death experience, leaving me a lot more grateful on this second Thanksgiving supper this holiday.

Every camper had their own fancy display with blowups, bales of hay, scarecrows, pumpkins, mums, and all sorts of different signs about fall and camping for the season.

It was spectacular to see how they all took the decoration contest so seriously. Dottie was taking her job as the judge very seriously. She was walking around to each campsite, giving all of the decorations a good once-over.

I swear she stood at each campsite long enough to smoke a full cigarette at each one of them. She even had them plug in their decoration lights that hung on the outsides of their campers to make sure each bulb was lit up.

She and Henry did a great job with the campground decorations. They'd put out small baskets next to each bale of hay and chair with blankets in them, because as soon as the sun went down, the temperatures would fall into the forties, and that would be around 6:00 p.m., which was just too darn early to turn in for the night.

Besides, Blue Ethel and the Adolescent Farm Boys wouldn't even take the small stage until around 7:00 p.m.

The recreational building was filled with children inside as they played games like cornhole, tic-tac-toe with beanbags, and some fall face painting by Abby.

"Are you okay?" I asked Betts after I found her sitting in an Adirondack chair on the dock. She was terribly quiet since she'd gotten here. "I'm surprised you even came."

Everyone knew Lester had died, and even though they weren't legally married anymore and he'd spent the last few years in prison, she still loved him.

"Lester and I had a conversation the other night." She tugged her legs up underneath her and pulled a blanket from the basket, placing it over her legs. "He said he knew he didn't have much time on this earth, so he wanted to help out where he could. He went to talk to Will, and he said Will brushed him off. But Will also talked about Christine and how he'd love for Lester to marry them."

Richard Will Denning had literally lost his mind. I'd heard from Agnes they'd already shipped Will to a mental facility to be evaluated, so I knew he wasn't in his right mind over the last few days. It still didn't give him a pass for what he'd done.

"He said he remembered all the people who came to him for help, confessions or whatever they needed when he was a preacher. He wrote them down in a small notebook while in prison." She pulled a small notebook out of her pocket. "Some of these are just people who needed a handout, and some of these requests are people who came to see him in prison."

She passed me the notebook, and I began to flip through it.

"He said he wanted to make everything right with these people, and Will was one of them. He knew Will was upset about Christine back when Theodore had died. He said he had an idea Will could've helped Theo on the trail from things Will had said, but when Jerry and Varney had come to the conclusion it was an accident, he let it go." She pointed to her chest. "He knew in here. That was Lester's greatest compass. His heart when something wasn't right."

"This is fascinating." I continued to thumb through the notebook and let Betts talk. It was as though she needed to sort things out in her head.

"Funny thing." She looked back at me.

I gave her back the notebook.

She rubbed the cover. "Lester joked that when the time came, he wanted me to slip lots of sleeping pills into his food so he died without pain and slipped away."

I guessed the only comfort she took from Colonel Holz's initial autopsy report from Lester's body was that the morphine Will gave him did let him pass peacefully.

"I have to believe Lester knew he was going to die from the shot and welcomed death." All her death talk was giving me the creeps, but I listened, or at least pretended to listen while I glanced around the campground.

I noticed the Riveras had showed up and were talking with some of the locals. I caught Ryan staring back at me from across the lake. He lifted his red cup up in the air with a slight nod.

Fifi and Chester were bounding about, going from campsite to campsite to see who was going to give them a little snack. Soon I was going to have to put them inside due to the fact the days were shorter and nightfall would be here.

Bobby Ray and Abby had emerged from the recreational building with a slew of kids trailing behind them as they made their way toward the mouth of Red Fox Trail. They were going to be good parents one day.

Mary Elizabeth was hanging out with some of the women from the Elks club. All of them appeared to have a piece of Mary Elizabeth's pie. No doubt she was using it to get herself into the club.

"I think I'll go through his notebook and finish out all the deeds he wanted to do." She had resigned herself to the fact that it was now her duty to fulfill Lester's dying wish.

"If you need any help, I'm more than happy to. You know that." I reached over and patted her hand. "You mean the world to me."

She looked up and smiled.

"Will you be one of my bridesmaids?" I knew this was a special time to ask her.

"I'd love to." She whispered thank you, as if it was what she needed at this moment to heal.

"I'll leave you to think. We have plenty of time to plan what on earth you're going to wear to my wedding." I placed my hand on my chest and batted my eyes with a little more of a twang in my voice than normal.

I made my way over to the firepit where Jerry and Emmalyn were talking to Hank.

They were talking about Christine's place and Jerry's almost-deadly experience. Though we were so glad the EMTs got there to reverse the overdose before it was deadly.

"There's just one thing that didn't add up." I glanced around the campground and stared across the lake at Betts when I watched Ryan Rivera make his way over to her.

Hank jumped up from his seat to offer it to me.

"I'm good. Sit. I'll pop a squat." I sat down in the grass and grabbed one of the blankets from the basket.

Will had burnt down the bakery to punish Christine after she'd rejected a pass from him the day before Thanksgiving, using me as an excuse to break away from the running team and not hurt his feelings. I accepted the fact he'd killed Garrett and Mitchell, because when he saw them at the Red Barn Restaurant that night, they were talking to Christine, and he was triggered back to the little boy who tried to tag along. That was what sent him down the killing spiral.

There was never going to be a time I'd understand the mind of a killer.

"Why did you send Mitchell death threats?" I looked between the Trumans.

"I can answer that." Emmalyn sat up. "It was me. I take full confession of it, and I'm not very good at these sorts of things, or else I'd not have showed you my glitter." She frowned. "Jerry had started to lose sleep a few weeks ago after he'd heard those boys were coming to town. Normally I'd tend to Garrett's mom's greenhouses when they are out of town, but since Garrett was coming into town, she said he was going to tend to them. She mentioned the boys and what happened years ago with Theo's investigation. She said it was all swept under the rug."

"In Emmalyn's defense, she didn't truly understand all of it until I told her. That's when she took it upon herself to send those nice letters, not really death threats if you read them." Jerry looked at Emmalyn.

"No, they were more along the lines of 'you better not bring up the past or else.' I didn't know what else it would be, but I certainly never thought it would come to what did transpire." Emmalyn, no matter how she put it, was wrong to write those notes, and I was sure Al wasn't done with her.

"I have a meeting with Al about it, and we are sure our lawyer will be able to get any charges dropped," Jerry assured her. "It'll all be fine."

Jerry reminded me of Hank.

Both wanted their significant others to feel warm and safe.

Both would do anything to make us happy.

Only time would tell if Al was going to bring any formal charges against Emmalyn, even though Will had confessed to and taken responsibility for all the murders with pride as Al had carted him off to jail from Christine's house.

Sounds of applause echoed around the campground in a wave. Everyone was turned to give Christine Watson a grand clap when she arrived.

"Excuse me." I left them and walked up to greet Christine. I'd not seen her or talked to her since our near-death experience. It was certainly an event that would bring us closer.

She was already talking to a few people when I finally made it up to the front of the campground. Fifi had already found her and was yipping at Christine's feet.

"Oh, Buck!" I heard Christine scream as I walked up, and she threw her arms around him.

"What?" I asked. "What are we celebrating?"

"You know the Tough Nickel Thrift Shop has all that extra space up top." Buck, the owner of the Tough Nickel Thrift Shop in downtown Normal, continued, "Since it was an old house back in the day like the rest of the cottages downtown, there was a kitchen up there that I never took out. I've offered the space for Christine to move the Cookie Crumble there until she gets back on her feet."

"And I accept." Christine knew as well as I did that this was a new beginning for her and our community.

"Perfect." I knew there had to be a silver lining in this Thanksgiving craziness.

"And to think when we were trapped in my media room, we thought it was all over." She looked at me with tears in her eyes.

We talked a few more minutes before she headed off to tell the rest of the locals the big news.

I couldn't help but notice Ryan was sitting in the Adirondack chair I'd just occupied a little while ago. Both Ryan and Betts had huge smiles on their faces. The blanket fell off Betts's legs, and he picked it up.

I watched them as their hands touched when she tried to take the blanket, but he tucked the edges underneath her legs. Her hand was placed on his bicep.

I smiled. The sweet gesture Ryan had done for her and her reaction sent my little matchmaking mind whirling.

"I reckon that smile is for Betts." Dottie's bedazzled turkey on her long-sleeved black shirt sparkled with the last bit of sun as it peeked over the mountain.

"I'm currently checking out the shirt." I laughed.

"Just you wait." She puffed out her chest. "These here are glow-in-the-dark beads. I'll be cock-a-doodle-dooing all over this place tonight."

I shook my head with a huge smile. There was never a dull moment around her.

"I asked Betts to be a bridesmaid too." I crossed my arms and looked to the pier, where Betts and Ryan really seemed to be enjoying themselves.

"By the looks of it, she might beat you to the altar." Dottie tapped out a cigarette from the case and stuck it in her mouth. "I ain't see Ryan Rivera in a long time. Time can be a tricky thang."

"What do you mean? When I've talked to him, he seems like a really nice guy." I certainly didn't need for Betts to get involved with someone who wasn't good for her.

"Nah. I mean time has been good to him. He's hotter than doughnut grease." Her cigarette bounced in between her lips in time with her brows.

"What's hotter than doughnut grease?" Christine Watson joined us.

"Ryan Rivera." Dottie said his name in a smooth way.

"What about Ryan?" Abby found her way over to us and walked up on our conversation.

"What are y'all talkin' 'bout?" Queenie sashayed her way into the circle.

"Betts." I shot a look back across the lake so they knew what I was seeing. "She seems to be enjoying the new company of Ryan Rivera."

"I hope she finds love again," Abby said.

All of us tilted our heads to look over at Betts and let out a collective sigh.

"Speaking of Lester." I knew we weren't really conversing about him, but it was implied. "He had written down a bunch of good deeds he wanted to do and unfortunately didn't get around to doing them. Betts let me see the notebook, and one of them was for the Gifts and Glamping Christmas campaign." I shrugged, reminding them of the winter festival the committee liked to put on to drive tourism during the winter months. "I think we can all volunteer for it."

"Now that I have my new temporary home to bake, I'd love to participate." Christine was still glowing from the offer from Buck to move her business there until she got back up on her feet. "Ken will be here to assess the damage and will get me a quote, but I figured it'd be way up into the spring before I will see any money to rebuild."

I knew she was talking about Ken, the same insurance man I had for the campground.

"You too?" Dottie's disapproval of Ken had lasted since the first day I'd hired him. "He's a slowpoke and never comes through unless May-bell-ine calls him a million times."

"Don't listen to her," I assured Christine when a look of worry crossed over her. "He will get right on it."

"I'll tell you what." Dottie pointed her lit cigarette directly at Christine. "Pee in one hand and wish he comes through in the other and see which one gets filled up the fastest."

Dottie walked away, leaving us hanging on one of her Dottie-isms.

"I don't understand a word that woman says, but somehow, she's always right." Abby shrugged and skirted off to find Bobby Ray.

Queenie, Christine, and I stood there watching as Blue Ethel and the Adolescent Farm Boys set up their band equipment.

My eyes slid over the campground one more time to take in the goodness all around.

Another Thanksgiving had come and gone, not without its challenges. We had endured more pain, more shame, more sorrow, more grief than we could possibly fathom, but there was something about next year's gathering around the campground that sat in my soul, telling me there were more good times ahead in the next season of life.

My heart knitted with love for each and every person gathered at Happy Trails Campground. And for these friends in my world, I knew I would never walk alone. The feeling of the season had hit me and hit me hard.

I was overflowing with gratitude and love.

The phone vibrated in my pocket, and I pulled it out, half expecting it to be a text from Hank saying he'd gotten Fifi and Chester and put them inside for the night.

"Hey, Ken," I greeted him when I answered, half surprised it was him. "Just as the universe would have it. I was just talking about you."

"I hate to tell you, but you're being sued." The joy and thankful feeling I was high on just a few seconds ago shot out of me like a cannon. "Or really, the campground."

"What?" I questioned my insurance man and blinked a few times in disbelief.

"I'll be in town over Christmas, and we can discuss all the particulars then. In the meantime, don't do anything if you get any emails or phone calls. Direct them to me as your insurance agent. We have lawyers who will handle this." He clicked off the phone.

"What's got you all wapper-jawed?" Dottie asked. I was in such a shock I'd not even heard her or smelled her smoke.

"Buckle up," I whispered and searched for every other single Laundry Club Lady. "I have a feeling we are in for a bumpy ride. I'm going to need everyone's help."

The holiday feeling was gone, but at least I had felt it for a brief moment, and I wasn't going to let anyone or any lawsuit ruin Christmas.

I'd let everyone have a good time tonight, but in the morning, I was going to call an emergency meeting of the Laundry Club Ladies.

Ken said he'd be here during Christmas. I was going to have this solved before he got here. Mark my words.

THE END

If you enjoyed reading this book as much as I enjoyed writing it then be sure to return to the Amazon page and leave a review.

Go to Tonyakappes.com for a full reading order of my novels and while there join my newsletter. You can also find links to Facebook, Instagram and Goodreads.

Keep reading for a sneak peek of the next book in the series. Gifts, Glamping, & Glocks is now available to purchase on Amazon or read for FREE in Kindle Unlimited.

Chapter One of Book Twenty Nine
Gifts, Glamping, & Glocks

"Deck the halls, fa-la-la, and all that stuff," Dottie Swaggert bemoaned from the bottom of the ladder she was holding on to while I strung red garland along the top of the tiki hut as a child ran past us on his way back to his family's camper.

"Dottie." I grabbed the top rung when she wobbled down below.

She gave a quiet snort in the back of her throat as she deliberately shook the ladder.

"I don't know why on earth you decided not to have peace on earth just like the Christmas season is supposed to be about," she retorted. "That big ole heart of yours puts all of us in this predicament."

"What predicament?" I carefully stapled the next piece of garland, making sure not to get my fingers in the way. "We are doing good. Lester had a great idea, and if it helps Betts to move on and feel good, we are going to do it."

Betts Hager was one of us.

A Laundry Club Lady.

We were a group of five friends who had so much in common— gossip, mostly—but what better way to bring five nosy women together? Betts owned the local laundromat we used to get together and just talk about things.

Again, gossip.

Recently, her ex-husband—only ex because he'd been sent to prison and pardoned by the governor—had passed away. He'd left a notebook that was full of requests from his church congregation he'd not been able to fulfill or things he'd left undone after he'd gone to prison but was on borrowed time from the big man in the sky due to an illness he wasn't going to get pardoned from.

"If hosting an event that gives children a wonderful Christmas is something we can do to help Betts cross that off the list, then we are going to do it." I sucked in a deep breath.

The cold Kentucky weather skittered into my nose and pricked my lungs. Slightly, I turned to get a view of the Happy Trails Campground from this level and smiled.

"And it makes the campground really pretty." I loved how the Christmas tree on the dock of the lake was shining from the multicolored Christmas lights.

Plus, there were all the mini trees on the cute floating platforms in the lake made by Henry Bryant, the campground handyman, and Beck Greer, the local teenager who worked with Henry for me.

They had cleverly strung solar lights around each little tree and mirror-ball ornaments so during the day, the balls reflected the sunlight as if the lights were on, and as soon as the sun started to descend behind the mountains in the Daniel Boone National Forest, the twinkly lights came on, giving a breathtaking and delightful addition to the decorations.

"Why on earth does Betts feel like she's the Jesus in his redemption?" Dottie had long not been a big fan of Lester's pardon. Though he was a man of the cloth before he went to prison, Lester wasn't able to escape the sin that put him there.

"Everyone needs forgiving," I reminded her, though she squirmed uncomfortably below. "How does that look?"

I decided to give up on trying to convince her the toy drive we were hosting was going to be a good thing for everyone in the community, not just to make Betts feel better.

Truth of the matter, Betts was doing the good deeds only because she felt like if Lester had those marked off, he'd be let into the great eternal as they'd preached to the masses at the Normal Baptist Church.

For some reason, she'd taken on the sins that stuck him in prison as her lot in life. At some point, we, the Laundry Club Ladies and I, were going to have to help her see that Lester's shame wasn't her cross to bear.

That would have to wait. We needed to get these Christmas decorations up and get the campground looking like the North Pole before the kids staying in Happy Trails Campground for the week and the kids in the community got here to give Santa their wish lists.

After all, Christmas was just a few weeks away, and Santa had to get those toys made.

"Have you seen Otis?" I asked once I got off the ladder to see how it looked myself even though Dottie had said it was fine.

"Fine," to me, meant it could be better. Fine to Dottie meant it was amazing.

Otis Gullett had come to me after he'd heard we were looking for someone to play Santa for the Gifts and Glamping Christmas, the name of our event. He didn't have any experience, but he sure did have the build, if you know what I mean.

"He was over yonder last time I saw him." Dottie gestured to the recreational building, where we had some indoor games for the kids inside, and for the outside, we had gotten a few of the stand-up heaters to keep guests warm while Ty Randal and his brothers served the food they'd donated from the Normal Diner.

When I said the entire town came out in order to make Gifts and Glampnig Christmas a success, they went above and beyond.

Not only had Happy Trails Campground filled up fast after we promoted it during the Thanksgiving holiday, but all of the available rooms at the Old Train Station Motel, the Milkery's bed-and-breakfast, and the campgrounds within twenty miles of us filled up as well.

"Well, if you see him, please tell him the costume is in bungalow three so he knows he can go in there and change," I told Dottie since she'd decided to take a smoke break, which meant she wasn't going to do any work until she thoroughly enjoyed the lit cigarette in her mouth.

"If he passes by here, I'll tell him." Dottie made herself comfortable inside the tiki hut on the chair we had there for Santa.

"And don't forget to get your costume on." My jaw tightened in anticipation of her response as I walked away, but surprisingly, she did not respond.

I hurried past the igloo Henry and Beck had made, nearly tripping over the three pigeons on ice skates. One by one, they fell like dominoes on the glass disguised as a little pond in one of the many displays they set up around the campground.

Dottie's under-her-breath snicker didn't go unnoticed.

I didn't dare look back to see her facial expression or even hand gestures if she made any, since I knew she felt like me falling over my own feet was warranted because I was asking her to dress like an elf for a couple of hours before we switched off.

It was part of being an employee. We all pitched in where needed.

"Fifi," I called out to my little poodle. She was adorable in her reindeer antlers on her head and sweater to match. Fifi loved all her sweaters and certainly didn't mind the antlers as you'd think.

I really did believe she understood how cute she was and liked all the attention she got from everyone she decided to give time to.

"Let's get in one more last walk." I talked to her as if she were my human child, and the way she always responded made me think she understood every word I said.

We started right there at the tiki hut along the road and would make our way around the lake. It was the last time I'd be able to check on the guests of the campground who had pulled or driven in their own campers or the guests who came and rented one of my campers.

They might need more things like wood for their firepits or essentials for living that I kept in the office. Happy Trails Campground was a full-hookup campground that we kept open all seasons, which was rare in the middle of the forest since our weather turned downright freezing.

Most campgrounds around these parts shut down for the season right after Halloween.

Now that our bungalows at the far end of the campground had heat, those really went fast for families who didn't want to rent a camper for their gatherings. Of course, the pitched-tent area of the campground, located off the side of the bungalows in a wooded patch, was closed due to the nature of that type of camping.

I didn't need anyone to get frostbite and die.

That wouldn't be good for business.

"I love your gingerbread cutouts!" I called to the first campsite we came to, where the couple had their fifth wheel all leveled, set up, and ready to go.

They had transformed the outside of their camper to look like a gingerbread house and used the icicle lights to appear like dripping icing.

"Let me know if you need anything." I waved goodbye to them and noticed Henry and Beck had already restacked new wood for the firepits.

The campground looked like the North Pole was in the middle of the Daniel Boone National Forest instead of up near the Arctic Ocean.

The next lot was a vacant mini travel trailer we owned. It was so cute but only had enough room for one or a couple. It rarely was rented out during any sort of holiday. During the rest of the year, the little camper was booked, more times than not by someone who was looking to come for a little break from life, reconnect with their soul, and just get away.

We offered the perfect getaway here at Happy Trails Campground with all the gorgeous trails that wound through the Daniel Boone National Forest, where you couldn't stop the soul growth even in you tried.

Plus, we offered many outdoor recreational sports like kayaking, canoeing, archery, hiking, and floating in the stream off the Red Fox Trail, as well as fishing and swimming in the lake right outside the campers.

I ran my hand along the plastic chain-link fence Henry had strung along the entire property of the campground. He'd brought me several photos he'd gotten online, showing he wanted to make the event into truly what kids would imagine the North Pole would look like, and he certainly had worked day and night since Thanksgiving to make it just so.

"It looks great." I walked up to the front of our small camper to see the finishing touches on the Santa's-office display that Henry had made in the vacant space.

"Thanks." He handed the garland to Beck. They'd made the fun spread from the fallen leaves and old vines he'd gathered from the forest. "It was Beck's idea after I showed him the photo."

The fireplace was fake and used gas logs and a propane tank that was hidden in the back of the stone fireplace they'd erected. They'd made a huge chimney and decorated the front of it with a framed photo of Santa's family, and that included the elves, reindeer, and Mrs. Claus.

There was a live Christmas tree next to the fireplace, all decorated and with wrapped presents below. Even Mrs. Claus had a rocking chair on the other side of the fireplace, where she had her balls of knitting yarn in a basket with a nice blanket draped over the back.

It was a perfect place to imagine her sitting there with the crackling fire while Santa sat behind the desk, where there was a nice list with big check marks next to names along with a big mug of coffee sitting next to it.

"It looks great, right?" Beck's excitement made his young and ever-so-changing teenager's voice go a pitch higher. "Wait until you see the fireworks."

He reddened from embarrassment, but I acted like I'd not noticed.

"Honestly, I really do feel like I've just stepped into Santa's office." I was amazed at how Henry made his images in his head come to life. "Thank you two for your hard work." I glanced around. "Where is the picnic table?" I wondered because those were stationary from the steel nails I'd had Henry drive into the concrete.

"Otis and I used his impact driver to take out the screws." Henry kept on working.

"Well, at least he did something," I moaned and pulled my phone out from my pocket and noticed we had under two hours until the charity event started.

"And the sleigh." I pointed up to the tiki hut, where he'd gotten a real sleigh from Buck, the owner of the Tough Nickel Thrift Shop. I had to take my mind off Otis.

From what I understood, Henry told Buck what he wanted, and

Buck found it and brought it here, where the donated toys were going to be placed during the event.

"It worked out perfect." Henry snorted and grinned big. His large nose flattened along his face, and the smile grew and exposed his missing front two teeth, but the pride on his face showed how much his efforts had come to life.

"If we get snow, I bet we can get Ms. Ogden to bring a couple of her horses here to pull us." Beck had the look of glee children get during the holidays, and it warmed my soul to be part of his new memories.

This was certainly going to be a Christmas to remember.

I knew it. I felt it deep in my bones.

"That would be something, if we got snow for that to happen." I could picture Beck's request and Coke Ogden, the owner of not only the Old Train Station Motel but a horseback riding experience she offered to tourists for trail rides and really putzing about.

"Have you seen Otis?" I asked Henry. "He really needs to start getting ready for his Santa debut."

"Probably stumbled into the woods, drunk." Beck snorted.

"Beck," I gasped. "Why would you say such a thing?" Not that I was his mama, but he certainly didn't act like the gossipy woman she was, even though I did hint around certain topics to Beck when I needed to know the answers to things because I knew his mama had her finger on the pulse of the gossip of various women's circles in Normal I wasn't privy to.

Beck pointed to Henry.

"I-ah... well... um," Henry spat out. "He is the town drunk now."

"Why would you say that?" I'd not heard this, but then again, I wasn't around Otis Gullett much either.

"I heard the men talking about it over cards. He's been hitting the bottle pretty good, and it's showing." Henry patted his gut, letting me know in his own way how Otis got the big belly that had reminded me of Santa when Otis asked if he could play the jolly guy. "I kept an eye on him today when he got here. I couldn't help but notice he was nipping in his car."

My brows pinched, and I glanced over my shoulder near the storage units located up front where I'd asked everyone to park so we could clear space for the locals' cars.

I didn't see Otis in his car, but it didn't mean he wasn't in there.

"If you see him, tell him to go to bungalow three to put his Santa outfit on." I shook my head.

The sound of gravel spitting up against an oncoming car had gotten my attention.

"Who on earth is that?" I questioned, knowing Hank Sharp, my fiancé, was at the entrance of the campground and not letting anyone drive up early. "Come on, Fifi."

I clicked my tongue, and when she rushed over, I picked her up.

I didn't recognize the car and wasn't sure if it was a guest of one of our campers, but nonetheless, I hurried around the perimeter of the campground, giving all the guests a quick glance to see if they needed anything before I put Fifi in our camper for a little rest before she made her big debut next to Santa as a helper.

As I came out of my camper, I realized the car had pulled up into my lot next to my little Ford.

"Ken, Magdalene," I greeted the Heidelmans. I was a bit shocked since he'd not let me know they were coming, even though they didn't really need to tell me since they rented a year-round spot in the campground near the back and next to the bungalows.

"Mae, we have to talk about this lawsuit." Ken was my insurance man and had practically ruined my Thanksgiving after he gave me the news I was being sued by a camper who'd stayed here the first year I was open due to a spider bite they'd gotten.

"Ken," I said flatly, "take a look around."

I drew my arms out in front of me.

"We are in the middle of the Daniel Boone National Forest. There are bugs, spiders, snakes, and even bears here. Those people took the kayaking class with Alvin Deters. They stopped along the stream and hiked, ate, and just relaxed on the banks. They could've been bitten anywhere."

"They have photos, Mae. They have photos of a spider in that camper." He pointed across the lake to Santa's office and the empty little travel trailer.

"I don't have time for this. I've got to find my Santa." I bent down and looked into the closed passenger's-side window where Magdalene was sitting. "Hi, Magdalene. You're going to love the food today! All campfire food."

She rolled down the window.

"I hope you've got some spiked cider. Ken needs it. He's been worried sick about this lawsuit, and I've told him everything you have." Her lips pinched. "He's driving me nuts."

"We really need to talk, Mae." Ken was right back on my heels.

"We will!" I called as I hurried toward the front of the campground, where I needed to see if Otis was in his car.

But Ken didn't stop. He kept following me.

"Ken, you have to let me get through today, and we will sit down in the morning." I laughed when I saw Magdalene crawl into the driver's seat and throw their car into drive and proceed to drive herself down to their camper.

"For now, I have to find Otis. Or we won't have a Santa." I stalked over to Otis's car, and sure enough, he was lying down in the seat with a silver flask resting on his chest.

I gave a few hard knocks on the window.

"Whaaaat?" Otis jerked up, his eyes closed.

"Otis Gullett! How on earth are you going to play Santa drunk?" My insides were as hot as the flaming firepits around the campground. My nose flared as it sucked the cold air in and condensation puffed out.

"Mae, can we now talk about the lawsuit?" Ken interrupted my anger at Otis and put the spotlight on himself.

"I'll make you a deal." I sighed with the thought. "I need a Santa, and you need my ear. The only way I can honestly get my head wrapped around the lawsuit today is to relax and de-stress so a wonderful event can take place so every child has a wonderful Christmas experience."

"What are you saying?" He was taking the cookies just like Santa does at each house he visits while delivering his presents.

"I need a Santa. You need my ear." I shrugged and watched Dottie walk up.

She leaned to look in the window at Otis. She lingered a while.

"You scratch my back, and I'll scratch yours." I told him in no uncertain terms that if he filled in for Otis as Santa, I'd give him all the time he needed to discuss the lawsuit.

"Fine." He gave me a hard look.

"You'll find the Santa outfit in bungalow three. Be ready in an hour." I smiled as he stormed back down the campground toward his camper. "There. Now I don't have to worry about Otis," I said, expecting Dottie to say something.

Silence.

"Dottie?" I turned my attention from Ken back to Dottie.

"Mm-hmm," she hummed, still looking into Otis's car window. "He's as useless as a milk bucket under a bull."

Little did I know, Dottie had hit the nail on the head about Otis, and soon, I was about to find out just how useless he was.

Gifts, Glamping, & Glocks is now available to purchase or in Kindle Unlimited.

RECIPES AND CAMPING HACKS FROM MAE WEST AND THE
LAUNDRY CLUB LADIES AT THE HAPPY TRAILS CAMPGROUND
IN NORMAL KENTUCKY.

Camping Hack #1

We are rolling into the fall and winter months with the release of Trappings, Turkeys, & Thanksgiving.

Did you know a lot of campgrounds are seasonal in the Midwest, south, and east due to the climate?

Some are open but if you use an RV, many times than not the campground has limited services which means you might not have water hookup or electric.

If you're like us, we love to camp year-round and have a few hacks that you need in order to enjoy camping or using your RV during the colder temperatures.

BATTERIES

Batteries do not work well in the cold. I know, I know, you put brand new batteries in your flashlight before you left home. BUT guess what, the flashlight isn't working. Before you replace your batteries, take them out and warm them up in your hands. Then put them back in. I bet your flashlight works again!

VENTS IN YOUR TENT

I know it makes perfect sense to keep the vents in your tent closed during the winter camping but don't! Leave them open.

Otherwise, your breath will condense, creating snow or water inside your tent.

WATER AND WATER BOTTLES

Even in the winter we have to drink water all the time while camping. You're in and out of the camper or tent, you're hiking trails and your body still needs to be hydrated. Keep your water bottles and water jugs upside down so they freeze at the bottom first.

Who would've ever thought? I picked this trick up from another camper after my water in my water bottle was frozen at the top but liquid at the bottle. This little hack with keep the water at the top liquid and drinkable!

What a great trick!

Dirty Chai Donuts: Christine Watson's recipe from Cookie Crumble

Ingredients
Donuts

- 1/2 cup milk (plant-based milk, or water)
- 1/2 cup oil or butter (melted)
- 3 eggs
- 1 1/2 teaspoons cinnamon, 1/2 teaspoon cardamom, and 1/4 teaspoon ginger
- 1 Box Vanilla Cake Mix

Dirty Chai Sugar

- 1 cup sugar
- 1 1/2 teaspoons cinnamon, 1/2 teaspoon cardamom, and 1/4 teaspoon ginger
- 1 teaspoon instant espresso granules
- 1/2 cup coconut oil (melted)

Equipment you will need

- Mini Muffin Pan

Directions

1. Preheat the mini muffin pan in the oven.
2. Whisk together milk, butter, eggs, cinnamon, cardamom, ginger, and Vanilla Cake Mix in a large bowl until smooth.
3. Fill the muffin tin.
4. Bake according to the vanilla cake mix directions on the box, or until donuts are golden brown.
5. Use a small spatula to remove finished donuts from the pan and set on a plate or rack to cool.

6. Make the Dirty Chai Sugar while the donuts are cooling.
7. Dip cooled donuts into melted coconut oil, then roll in dirty chai mixture.

Camper Hack #2

Winter Campfire Hack

Having a fire going during the fall and winter months is crucial!

Take a small square of foil, a cotton ball coated with Vaseline, and fold the cotton/vaseline soaked ball into the foil in a small square. When it's time to start the fire, cut an X in the packet and twist out a small amount of cotton into a wick and strike a spark to it. It will light dependably first time, every time. It will last up to 10–15 minutes depending on how much vaseline you put in the cotton.

Works like a charm each time and you don't have to worry if you'll be able to sit by a fire and warm your cold toes!

Autumn Fizz

Ingredients

2 oz Alibi Gin

.25 oz lemon juice

Agave nectar, to taste

Sparkling apple cider

Garnished with apple

Directions

- Pour gin in shaker,
- add lemon juice and agave nectar,
- shake, and then
- pour into a high ball glass and
- top with sparkling cider.
- Garnish with an apple slice.

A NOTE FROM TONYA

Thank y'all so much for this amazing journey we've been on with all the fun cozy mystery adventures! We've had so much fun and I can't wait to bring you a lot more of them. When I set out to write about them, I pulled from my experiences from camping, having a camper, and fond memories of camping.

Readers ask me if there's a real place like those in my books. Sadly, no. It's a combination of places I've stayed and would own if I could.
    XOXO ~ Tonya

For a full reading order of Tonya Kappes's Novels, visit
Tonyakappes.com

BOOKS BY TONYA
SOUTHERN HOSPITALITY WITH A SMIDGEN OF HOMICIDE

Camper & Criminals Cozy Mystery Series

All is good in the camper-hood until a dead body shows up in the woods.

BEACHES, BUNGALOWS, AND BURGLARIES
DESERTS, DRIVING, & DERELICTS
FORESTS, FISHING, & FORGERY
CHRISTMAS, CRIMINALS, AND CAMPERS
MOTORHOMES, MAPS, & MURDER
CANYONS, CARAVANS, & CADAVERS
HITCHES, HIDEOUTS, & HOMICIDES
ASSAILANTS, ASPHALT & ALIBIS
VALLEYS, VEHICLES & VICTIMS
SUNSETS, SABBATICAL AND SCANDAL
TENTS, TRAILS AND TURMOIL
KICKBACKS, KAYAKS, AND KIDNAPPING
GEAR, GRILLS & GUNS
EGGNOG, EXTORTION, AND EVERGREEN
ROPES, RIDDLES, & ROBBERIES
PADDLERS, PROMISES & POISON
INSECTS, IVY, & INVESTIGATIONS
OUTDOORS, OARS, & OATH
WILDLIFE, WARRANTS, & WEAPONS
BLOSSOMS, BBQ, & BLACKMAIL
LANTERNS, LAKES, & LARCENY
JACKETS, JACK-O-LANTERN, & JUSTICE
SANTA, SUNRISES, & SUSPICIONS
VISTAS, VICES, & VALENTINES
ADVENTURE, ABDUCTION, & ARREST
RANGERS, RVS, & REVENGE

CAMPFIRES, COURAGE & CONVICTS
TRAPPING, TURKEY & THANKSGIVING
GIFTS, GLAMPING & GLOCKS
ZONING, ZEALOTS, & ZIPLINES
HAMMOCKS, HANDGUNS, & HEARSAY
QUESTIONS, QUARRELS, & QUANDARY
WITNESS, WOODS, & WEDDING
ELVES, EVERGREENS, & EVIDENCE
MOONLIGHT, MARSHMALLOWS, & MANSLAUGHTER
BONFIRE, BACKPACKS, & BRAWLS

Killer Coffee Cozy Mystery Series

Welcome to the Bean Hive Coffee Shop where the gossip is just as hot as the coffee.

SCENE OF THE GRIND
MOCHA AND MURDER
FRESHLY GROUND MURDER
COLD BLOODED BREW
DECAFFEINATED SCANDAL
A KILLER LATTE
HOLIDAY ROAST MORTEM
DEAD TO THE LAST DROP
A CHARMING BLEND NOVELLA (CROSSOVER WITH MAGICAL CURES MYSTERY)
FROTHY FOUL PLAY
SPOONFUL OF MURDER
BARISTA BUMP-OFF
CAPPUCCINO CRIMINAL
MACCHIATO MURDER

Holiday Cozy Mystery Series

CELEBRATE GOOD CRIMES!

FOUR LEAF FELONY
MOTHER'S DAY MURDER
A HALLOWEEN HOMICIDE
NEW YEAR NUISANCE
CHOCOLATE BUNNY BETRAYAL
FOURTH OF JULY FORGERY
SANTA CLAUSE SURPRISE
APRIL FOOL'S ALIBI

Kenni Lowry Mystery Series

Mysteries so delicious it'll make your mouth water and leave you hankerin' for more.

FIXIN' TO DIE
SOUTHERN FRIED
AX TO GRIND
SIX FEET UNDER
DEAD AS A DOORNAIL
TANGLED UP IN TINSEL
DIGGIN' UP DIRT
BLOWIN' UP A MURDER
HEAVENS TO BRIBERY

Magical Cures Mystery Series

Welcome to Whispering Falls where magic and mystery collide.

A CHARMING CRIME
A CHARMING CURE
A CHARMING POTION (novella)
A CHARMING WISH

BOOKS BY TONYA

A CHARMING SPELL
A CHARMING MAGIC
A CHARMING SECRET
A CHARMING CHRISTMAS (novella)
A CHARMING FATALITY
A CHARMING DEATH (novella)
A CHARMING GHOST
A CHARMING HEX
A CHARMING VOODOO
A CHARMING CORPSE
A CHARMING MISFORTUNE
A CHARMING BLEND (CROSSOVER WITH A KILLER COFFEE
COZY)
A CHARMING DECEPTION

Mail Carrier Cozy Mystery Series

Welcome to Sugar Creek Gap where more than the mail is being delivered.

STAMPED OUT
ADDRESS FOR MURDER
ALL SHE WROTE
RETURN TO SENDER
FIRST CLASS KILLER
POST MORTEM
DEADLY DELIVERY
RED LETTER SLAY

About Tonya

Tonya has written over 100 novels, all of which have graced numerous bestseller lists, including the USA Today. *Best known for stories charged with emotion and humor and filled with flawed characters, her novels have garnered reader praise and glowing critical reviews. She lives with her husband and a very spoiled rescue cat named Ro. Tonya grew up in the small southern Kentucky town of Nicholasville. Now that her four boys are grown men, Tonya writes full-time in her camper she calls her SHAMPER (she-camper).*

Learn more about her be sure to check out her website tonyakappes.com. Find her on Facebook, Twitter, BookBub, and Instagram

Sign up to receive her newsletter, where you'll get free books, exclusive bonus content, and news of her releases and sales.

If you liked this book, please take a few minutes to leave a review now! Authors (Tonya included) really appreciate this, and it helps draw more readers to books they might like. Thanks!

Made in the USA
Las Vegas, NV
13 November 2024

11769807R00115